ONE

The massive doors were unlocked, but it took both hands and all her strength to tug one open. Squinting into the dark interior, Gayle let the door close behind her. On a sunny day, the stained-glass panels would light the lobby with dazzling colors, but the rain left them murky and lifeless.

Even in the dim light, the space was astonishing. She'd never been inside the theater in the daytime, without the brilliant chandeliers and chattering voices. It was more lavish and extravagant now that she could see it all, without the crowds of theatergoers. The grand staircase, guarded by stylized, scowling lions, rose majestically to the mezzanine level before splitting into two curving flights. The lions looked less imposing now than they'd appeared with the lights gleaming on the gilded marble and sparking their ruby eyes.

"We're closed."

Gayle jumped and peered up, barely discerning a small woman leaning over a balcony two stories above. "Good morning."

"We're closed," she repeated. "Come back at twelve-thirty for the matinee. If you're with the show, use the Clover Street door." The woman shook out a long-handled feather duster, and Gayle stepped back to avoid the cascade of dirt.

"I have an appointment with Mr. Hewitt Langdon."

"Appointment at eight o'clock in the morning?" The woman scoffed. "I don't know where he'd be at eight o'clock in the morning."

"I'm right here, Ernie, because I have an appointment." The man emerging from the depths of the lobby was short and thick, with a voice to match. "Are you Miss Wells?"

"Yes, sir." She controlled the absurd urge to curtsy and held out her hand instead. "Gayle Wells."

"Nice to meet you." He looked up at the housekeeper. "Are you cleaning or just rearranging the dust, Ernie?"

"I'm worn to the bone, that's what I'm doing." Ernie slapped the balcony rail. "That daft girl you hired yesterday is useless. She dropped one of those vases in the back of the foyer, and only Providence stopped it from smashing. I set her to hoover the mezzanine. She can't break the floor."

Gayle pitied the girl. The Empire was known for its valuable—and breakable—treasures. Newspapers had run feature stories on the collection, with an emphasis on how portable the items were, as if inviting thieves to have a crack at it.

The theater manager sighed dramatically. "Mr. Starek is reconsidering the placement of the vases. And everything else." He glowered at a small statue of an Egyptian queen. Her aloof expression didn't change. "So, Miss Lady Organist, let's find Frank and get you your audition."

Miss Lady Organist? Gayle compressed her lips and followed him through the lobby. She was qualified for this job, graduating from Eastman School of Music with a certificate in film accompaniment. That was more than most theater organists had, but she was a woman, and if Lillian Nagle hadn't asked Mr. Langdon to give her an audition, she might not have been given a chance to prove her ability. Mother was right…it was a man's world.

He turned down a wide hall lined with velvet-covered benches. "My office is down here. Frank's is in the basement."

Gayle wasn't sure who Frank was or why his office was in the basement, or even why they were looking for him, but she was glad she'd worn her organ-playing shoes. Not only did they match her best suit and cloche, they were also good for climbing stairs and walking long halls. She kept up easily as Langdon descended two sets of carpeted steps, walked across a tiled landing, and opened a heavy wood door. The hallway beyond was covered with linoleum.

Langdon knocked on the first door before trying the knob. Locked. He huffed and continued down the hall. "I told him to be here at eight. Probably in the rehearsal hall. Around the back, of course." Another exaggerated sigh. "Come along."

The manager was breathing audibly by the time they reached the rehearsal hall. Two men with pomaded dark hair and small mustaches leaned against an organ and smoked thin cigarettes. Another sat on the bench, his sour expression a contrast to their merriment.

Langdon glared at them. "I thought you were meeting us in your office."

The nearest man, tall and thin, shrugged. "Seemed unnecessary. We'd have just walked right back here."

"They've been devising a test," said his companion. He looked at Gayle with an impudent smirk. "To see if the girl organist is any good."

The girl organist. Gayle dug her fingernails into her palms, trying to think of a mature response.

"To see how she handles different situations," the man hurried on. "Fast and slow film. Drama and comedy. That kind of thing. Some concert music and accompaniment."

"Get outta here." Langdon stepped aside and waited for the man to slide past him.

"I just needed some direction. I'll be up in the booth, running the film."

Langdon shut the door behind the projectionist. "Miss Wells, may I present Frank Bennet, music director, and our master organist, Jesse Erwin. Frank is the one you have to impress. And Jesse, of course."

Jesse scowled. He stood, waving at the bench. "Have a seat." He managed to infuse sarcasm into the three short words. Gayle sat, hoping she appeared confident and pleasant instead of anxious and annoyed.

AN HOUR LATER, she was seething. The men had had a grand time testing her. The projectionist played the film fast and then slowed unexpectedly before speeding up again, without regard for the score. She almost missed the changes in the flickering screen. When he suddenly switched to a different movie, without even a cue sheet, she had to improvise.

The solo pieces weren't a problem. Her confidence increased until Mr. Bennet dropped a stack of songbooks on the bench.

"New songs, just out, from that new show in New York." He pointed at the top one. "That one first." Gayle picked it up, flipped it open, and studied the page. Complicated. She'd been playing accompaniment forever, but she'd never even heard this song before. She kept up fairly well, ignoring Jesse Erwin's rude commentary.

When the director told her to stop, she nodded confidently. She'd done the best she could, and no man could have done better. She deserved the job.

"So? Will she do?" Mr. Langdon appeared impatient.

Mr. Bennet looked at Jesse. "I suppose so. Jesse?"

The organist shrugged. "She ain't no Rosa Rio, but she'll do for matinees and some of the smaller shows."

Of course, she wasn't Rosa Rio. She would be as good, though, once she'd been performing as long as the other woman. "Miss Rio was very kind to me at Eastman School of Music," she said. "She's married to one of my professors."

"That's right. You went to Eastman. Some of our orchestra went there. Maybe you know them." Bennet mentioned a few names, as if testing her further.

Gayle shook her head. "I wasn't there for a degree. I just did the film accompaniment program. I learned to play the organ at church."

"What church?" Jesse demanded.

"Second Presbyterian on fifth and Dearborn."

He grunted. "Good organ."

It was an excellent organ, and she'd been playing it for most of her life. Papa had let her play on it while he worked in his office, warning her that she'd get in trouble if the choir director caught her. When Gayle turned ten, he hired the choir director to teach her how to play it properly.

"Be here at seven tomorrow," Bennet said. "The new film, *Bluff*, starts on Friday, and the score's a mess. We'll work on that for a while, and then you can practice with the orchestra at ten." He picked up the songbooks. "Watch Jesse at the matinee for *Between Friends*, and then come back to watch the evening show. You'll have to work hard if you're going to be ready for Friday."

"Oh, no, you don't." The organist shook his head. "You know you can't do that. She may not be a member of the federation yet, but she will be, and you have to follow the rules."

"She's just watching, not performing," Langdon said. "Not working."

Jesse turned to Gayle. "Don't let them talk you into working all day, and watching is working. I'll give you a copy of the federation's guidelines later and get you signed up."

"I'm already a member," she said. "I joined during college, even before I went to Eastman. I was doing some performing back then."

"Good, good. You'll have to stand up for your rights around here." The organist might not approve of her, but he wasn't going to let the management push her around.

"Well," said Bennet, "when do you think she should work?"

Jesse leaned against the organ, ignoring the music director's sarcastic tone. "She should get in on the start of rehearsals for *Bluff*, but one hour before the orchestra gets here should be enough. Then she can come back for the evening show. It's a big one, with the Ingenues before the vaudeville acts, and *Between Friends* is a long film."

The other men nodded. Apparently, Jesse had authority—or maybe it was the union. Either way, she was in. None of them seemed to be happy about it. Maybe men didn't get excited about such things, or maybe they honestly weren't impressed by her audition. She'd have to prove herself over time, and they'd come to appreciate her talents eventually. She hoped.

"See? After all your grumbling, your union membership paid off!" Gayle's mother beamed, clasping her hands in front of her as if in prayer—probably in gratitude that her shiftless daughter was finally doing something worthwhile.

"I don't grumble about it," Gayle objected, "except for paying the dues when I wasn't even working as a musician." She pulled a bottle of milk from the icebox and handed it to her sister. "Besides, I got the job before the federation was even mentioned."

"If you become active in the union," her mother said, "you could make a real difference in the world!"

Gayle chuckled. "In the musicians' world?"

"Certainly! Musicians deserve good working conditions, too, and some of them have families to feed." After Cora

Wells's unflagging zeal as a suffragette and her years with the Christian Women's Temperance Union had been crowned with success, she always kept an eye open for new targets for her crusading skills. "And really," she said, "just being in that position will set a precedent for other women organists. You are a trailblazer."

Gayle grinned. "I'm not running for president, Mom. I'll leave world-changing to you and Dot. I'm just playing the organ at the Empire. They already have women in the orchestra."

"You could go on to be a famous composer or a college professor at that school you attended in New York," Dot said.

"Not with a six-month certificate in theater organ," Gayle said, "and I don't want to. That's why I went there—to play the organ. I won't even be the chief organist for a long time yet—if ever. In the meantime, I can pick up some other gigs at weddings, churches, or concerts to make extra money. I can give lessons, too."

"Gigs?" her mother asked. "Just what is a gig?"

"It's a word I learned at my one-and-only union meeting. It means job. Usually a short-term job."

"The Empire will be a long-term job, won't it?" Dot asked.

"Yes, I hope so," Gayle said. "It'll be fun. Maybe I'll even be a master organist someday, but I need to make a lot of money now if I'm going to save up enough for a car."

Gayle pulled an apron over her head and tied the strings. She hoped it would be a fun job. Today's experience had left her feeling deflated. At school, they'd all been enthusiastic about being in show business. It seemed more exciting than being a serious professional musician. Gayle liked music, but she'd lacked the drive for that. Two years at college hadn't inspired a burning passion to become a social activist, politician, doctor, or journalist either. It wasn't that she didn't find those things interesting. She found everything interesting. She just didn't want to restrict herself to only one thing.

Her mother handled Gayle's shortcomings with fortitude, pinning her hopes on her youngest daughter. At 21, Dot was shaping up to be a firebrand worthy of her mother, member of a dozen social, academic, and charitable organizations. Her sisters found her fervor annoying.

"You'll probably meet interesting people at the theater. Helen Keller and Annie Sullivan have been touring with a vaudeville act for a couple years." Dot sniffed. "It's ridiculous that they have to be associated with acrobats and trained monkeys."

Gayle opened the box of American cheese and started slicing. "Are they dancers?"

"Dancers!" Dot stopped to stare at her. "They're speakers. Helen Keller is blind and deaf, and Annie Sullivan is her teacher."

"That doesn't sound like a very exciting act," Gayle said. "Is the soup ready? I don't want to put the cheese toast in the oven until the last minute."

"Yes, but Papa isn't home yet. He had a meeting with the presbytery." Their mother pushed aside the curtain and peered out the window. "I thought he'd be finished by now."

"I bet he wishes he was," Gayle said. "Committee meetings are the worst."

"Here he is! Put that in the oven, Gayle, or he'll be waiting. Are you done setting the table, Dot?" As liberated as she claimed to be, their mother was the epitome of wifehood and homemaking. She removed her apron, patted her hair into place, and hurried to open the door. "He doesn't look happy."

TWO

Gayle used the Clover Street entrance this time, with a certain thrill of belonging. She was in show business now. She was also lost. A long hallway, abandoned at this time of the morning, stretched into the darkness. The designers hadn't spent money on this utilitarian part of the theater. Bare bulbs, set too far apart, made forlorn puddles of light on the gray floor. Gayle stepped forward uncertainly, wishing she'd left the building this way after her audition. A series of doors, labeled with numbers and no further information, ran the length of the corridor. Dressing rooms?

The hallway ended in a heavy fire door. Gayle turned the knob, and the door opened slightly before catching in a heavy velvet curtain. Was that legal? The exits were supposed to be open, in case of fire. She pushed her way through and found herself on the landing of a twisting staircase. As ornate as any of the other public areas, this staircase featured bas-relief medallions of elephants in gilded oval frames, ascending and descending in line with the steps. The walls were painted twilight blue, and gold drapes covered what might be another door, as they did the one she had just passed through. All for a back staircase.

Gayle headed down the stairs, marveling at the oriental carpet. The rehearsal hall and Mr. Bennet's office had been in the basement, but the Clover Street door hadn't opened onto the same level as the front door. Or did it? She continued past the second landing, down two more flights of stairs, until they ended abruptly in front of another gold drapery. Savvy now, she found the knob and pulled. Locked. She knocked, but no one responded. Sighing, she returned to the previous landing, which had no door at all behind the drapery, and then up one more level. The door opened easily, and bright lights and noise hit her like a wall after the hushed confines of the staircase.

"Outta the way, sister." A man ran in front of her, pulling a wagon full of coiled ropes. She seemed to be backstage, on the linoleum floors again, and still lost. Was there a map to this place?

She pulled the door closed and surveyed the hectic scene. A bald man approached with long strides, blue eyes narrowed, mouth bracketed with creases. He waved a clipboard at her. "Were you in that staircase?"

"Yes. I'm afraid I'm lost." Gayle tried to chuckle, but it came out more like a cough. "I was trying to find Mr. Bennet's office."

"Frank Bennet?" He regarded her for a few seconds. "Does he know you're coming?"

"He's expecting me."

He pointed across the stage with his clipboard. "Go as far as you can that way and turn left at the end. Then right and down three doors."

Gayle tromped away, certain she was heading back to where she'd started.

"Don't use these stairs," he called after her. "Use the stairs at the end of the hall by the offices."

The door to Mr. Bennet's office was closed and locked. Gayle shifted her leather portfolio bag higher on her shoulder and went in search of him. She was only two minutes late!

It occurred to her that the decor of the theater might be a reflection of the status of the people in each area. The linoleum of the back hallways and nether regions gave way to carpeting in the hall outside the music staff's offices. It lacked the elegance and depth of that in the public areas, but it was an agreeable green with a simple pattern of ivory circles. Pictures of famous musicians hung on the walls, but the frames weren't ornate and gilded. Considerable thought had gone into the architecture and decor of the Empire.

"What are you doing here?"

Her musings evaporated at the sound of Jesse Erwin's voice. "I'm here to start rehearsals."

He shook his head. "Bennet said you haven't filled out the paperwork yet, so you're not on the payroll."

"What paperwork?" Gayle let her portfolio fall to the floor. "He told me to be here at nine to go over the score for *Bluff*."

"Well, you have to fill out the employment paperwork before you can set foot in the rehearsal hall."

"Where's Mr. Bennet?" Gayle asked.

"Dunno." He turned to go. "I'd better get started on the *Bluff* score."

Exasperated and a little worried, she followed him. "Can I go with you and fill out the paperwork afterward?"

"Nope. You gotta do the paperwork," he said, "and you need to do that with Langdon, not Bennet."

"But I need to let Mr. Bennet know I'm here!" Gayle looked around. "I could just sit and watch you until he arrives." Would he respond to flattery? "You could help me with the score as well as he could, I'm sure."

"Sorry, that's Bennet's job, not mine." Jesse folded his arms across his chest. "See, that's what the unions are all about. We do our job, management does their job, the cleaning lady does her job, the ushers do their job, everyone does their jobs, and it all works out. No one person gets taken advantage of, and everyone keeps their jobs. But you gotta get the job before I can help you."

"I have the job." Gayle wanted to stamp her foot. "He said so yesterday. He told me to be here at nine. Do you have any idea where he is?"

"Haven't seen him." Jesse said. "Maybe he's with Langdon, waiting for you in his office."

"That's on the main level, right?" Upstairs and across the theater, no doubt.

"Yep. Good luck."

She watched him walk away, his pace more rapid than seemed natural. He was probably trying to get away from her.

"Can I help you?"

Gayle spun, startled. "I didn't see you there."

The man smiled, stylish in a yellow shirt and blue and white striped jacket. He wore a white bow tie and had a straw boater tucked under his arm, as if he'd just stopped by on his way to some sporting event. One of the vaudeville troupe? He was certainly handsome enough to be an actor.

"How could you? I hid around the corner until the organist left. I've never met such a quarrelsome man."

"I've only met him twice," Gayle said.

"And?"

"I don't know him well enough to say." And she didn't know this man at all. He might be Jesse Erwin's best friend, for all she knew, and Gayle wasn't going to say anything that might jeopardize her future.

"Take my word for it, then," the man said. "I'm scared to death of him. I'm afraid I'll sell three thousand tickets to a show, and then do something wrong, and he'll walk out on strike." He held out his hand. "I'm John Starek."

She should have recognized him from the pictures in the newspapers. They called him the Emperor, for no apparent reason other than his ownership of the Empire. He looked younger in person. She shook his hand. "I'm Gayle Wells, the new organist."

"Really?" He shot a hopeful glance down the hall, and Gayle hastened to clarify.

"The second organist. For matinees and some evening shows, to fill in when Mr. Erwin isn't available."

"I thought we already had a second organist. Um…" He squeezed his eyes shut, obviously thinking hard. After a few seconds, he clapped his hands in triumph. "Glassman. Henry, I think. What happened to him?"

Gayle picked up his hat and returned it to him. "He died in a car accident," she said. "Last week." At the sight of his stricken expression, she winced, regretting her casual response. "I'm sorry. I…"

"No one told me." He rubbed his forehead. "I was up in Lake Geneva last week, but they could have called me or sent a telegram."

For a second organist? She dredged up some conventional responses. A minister's daughter should have these skills. "My condolences. I am sorry for your loss."

"Not a loss. I mean, I didn't know him well at all, but as his employer, I should have been notified. We would have checked to make sure his family was provided for."

For a second organist? Maybe he was a social reformer like her mother. "I believe he was unmarried," Gayle said. "Jesse said something about it yesterday."

Actually, Jesse had said that if Henry had been more careful, he wouldn't have stepped in front of a fast car. Then they wouldn't have had to hire a new organist in such a hurry.

"Still, Langdon or his assistant should have informed me." After a few seconds, he continued. "So, based on the conversation I overheard, eavesdropping, you're looking for Langdon."

"I suppose so. I was looking for Mr. Bennet, but I guess I have to fill out paperwork for employment before I can start rehearsing for the new show."

"I saw Bennet by the back staircase a little while ago. Erwin will tell him you're here. Langdon's probably up in his office. I don't think he ever goes home." He beckoned her to follow him down the hallway. "I'll help you find him."

Gayle looked around, wishing the men would appear. She needed to meet with Mr. Bennet, not annoy him by going over his head and involving Mr. Starek.

He spoke over his shoulder, as if reading her mind. "I'd go with you to the rehearsal hall and tell them to get you started, but Erwin would jump all over that. Everything has to be done in order. Besides, I want to see Langdon, too."

She followed him along increasingly impressive halls and open spaces until they came to the manager's office. He wasn't there. The assistant manager's office was locked, too.

"Let's go to my office, and I'll call around and see if I can find him." He tipped his head toward the grand staircase and strode off. She trailed behind until they reached his office on the mezzanine level.

"Here it is." He held the door for her.

Gayle stopped in the doorway and blinked. In here, the fantastical decor seemed…a bit too much. Mr. Starek was obviously proud of it, though, so Gayle murmured appreciatively and entered the room. Her feet sank into the thick carpet as she walked across to the stained-glass window. Peering through the panes, she realized that the loss of the view was no sacrifice.

"The Halstead House is an excellent hotel, but I don't want to look into their windows—and I don't want them looking into my office." He sat at his desk—an enormous slab of marble on carved wood legs resembling dragons—and picked up the telephone handset. "We have an automated house phone, you know. No need for switchboard operators."

Gayle smiled at the boy-like pride in his voice as she explored the office. The ceiling was carved and painted like a cathedral's, with faceted globe chandeliers—twelve of them—

to compensate for the lack of light from the windows. She counted six doors, all with carved wood, stained-glass transoms, and ornate hardware. One for the secretary, one to the hallway, one to the bathroom. Maybe the others were closets or meeting rooms. A direct staircase? A hidden passageway? She wouldn't be a bit surprised.

Yellow velvet armchairs faced a fireplace that must be ornamental rather than functional. The risk of ash and smoke would be too great for the fine furnishings. Shelves of books flanked the fireplace, with smooth gilded spines very unlike her father's shabby library.

In the far corner, a gray-streaked marble statue rose nearly four feet from its base. Scraps of marble drapery protected the angel's modesty, but it still looked embarrassed. Gayle averted her eyes.

"No one is answering their phones—not even Miss Fisher, the assistant manager. She's always here from nine to six, like clockwork. No one answered in the downstairs offices either. Langdon must be here somewhere, though. He comes in early and stays through the last show and cleanup." He stood and strode toward the hallway door. "We'll find him. Come on."

Gayle dug her heels into the carpet and shook her head. "Maybe I should just wait in his office. Outside of it. I can't chase him all over the theater."

"You're supposed to start rehearsals, aren't you? Let's find him and get you started."

"I think I'd better wait for him." Her heart sank. She didn't want to lose this job—either because she couldn't get the paperwork done in time to start rehearsals or because she annoyed him by chasing him all over the theater in the company of the theater owner. Of the two options, waiting outside his office seemed safer.

GAYLE EYED the gilded chair dubiously. The dainty piece, with its red velvet cushion and diamond tufting, looked uncomfortable and alarmingly fragile. A few minutes on her feet wouldn't kill her. Breaking a fancy chair might. She'd checked her watch every few minutes since John Starek left her. The assistant manager was proving to be as elusive as Langdon was.

When she finally arrived, Gayle shifted from one foot to the other, trying not to fidget in the awkward waiting period as the woman approached, striding the length of the dim hallway. The assistant's boxy coat and the brim of her felt hat concealed her entirely, but her haste was apparent as she walked past Gayle, speaking over her shoulder as she unlocked the door.

"You must be Gayle Wells. I apologize for the delay." She didn't make excuses but held the door open so Gayle could enter.

"Yes. I'm supposed to meet with Mr. Langdon, but I can't find him. No one can find him. Everyone says he's always here early, but…" Gayle forced herself to stop chattering.

The other woman wasn't listening. She'd walked to the corner of the room, her back to Gayle, and was divesting herself of the gray coat. She hung it on a hook and smoothed the beaver collar before using both hands to lift the cloche. Her hair was probably meant to have smooth finger waves, but rebellious curls sprang from her head—not frizzy, but not fashionably sleek. In spite of the woman's brisk demeanor and severely professional blouse and skirt, the curls gave her a cherubic appearance.

"I have the contract ready for you. It's a standard agreement for a temporary employee, and it meets your union's specifications."

"Temporary?" Gayle's heart sank. "I understood it's a permanent job."

"And it will be," the woman said, "if your performance is satisfactory for three months."

"I think I should talk to Mr. Langdon before I sign that. I definitely understood this was a permanent job," Gayle said, "and I'm supposed to be at the rehearsal already. Do you know when or where I can find him?"

An odd expression crossed the woman's face. Irritation? No, it looked more like worry. "Mr. Langdon trusts me with these matters. I'm offering you a temporary job. A trial. If you don't want it, I am sure there are others who do."

Did this woman really have that authority? She turned at the sound of rapid steps in the hallway, hoping to see Langdon. Instead, John Starek filled the doorway.

"Good morning, Miss Fisher. I'm looking for Langdon. No one's seen him today at all."

"He's not here." The assistant tried to smooth a curl behind her ear. It bounced out again. "But I have everything under control."

"I'm sure you do, but I want to talk to Langdon. Why wasn't I told that Henry Glassman died?"

The question seemed to startle her. "Henry Glassman? The organist?" She glanced at Gayle before returning her attention to him. "I should have informed you. I'm sorry. It won't happen again."

"It wasn't your fault. Langdon should have called me. I want to see him when he arrives." He turned to Gayle. "You're still waiting for him, too?"

"I am. I'm supposed to complete paperwork before I start rehearsal, but Miss Fisher…" She paused, uncertain how to explain.

"I have the contract ready for her."

"It's a contract for a temporary job," Gayle said. "Mr. Langdon never said anything about it being temporary."

Starek frowned. "Is that customary? I've never heard Langdon talk about temporary jobs before. Is it because she's female? I was just down in the musician's lounge and heard some comments about that."

"Of course not!" Miss Fisher snapped. "It's a trial period, to be sure we aren't stuck with unsuitable employees. Male or female!"

"I don't know. Employees are Langdon's responsibility, of course, but it seems unreasonable to expect someone to take a job without knowing if it will last. Tell him I want to talk to him as soon as he gets back. Get Miss Wells a regular contract. I think we can trust her to be...er...suitable." He flashed a white smile at Gayle. "They're waiting for her down in the rehearsal hall."

She did her best to look respectable and trustworthy. "Thank you, sir."

He nodded at Miss Fisher, who compressed her lips and opened a file drawer. Gayle thought she might be grinding her teeth. It really was unfair to blame the woman for her boss's actions, if Mr. Langdon had indeed been responsible for the contract. Gayle wasn't sure of that. Miss Fisher had made it sound like she was personally offering Gayle the job, not doing it at Langdon's direction.

"It was nice to meet you, Miss Wells. Welcome to the Empire." Mr. Starek smiled at her again, nodded to Miss Fisher and left the office.

Gayle turned back to the assistant manager, who snatched away the first contract and rolled a new one into the typewriter. Gayle hoped she hadn't made an enemy on her first day at her new job.

Gayle hurried across the lobby, wishing she had time to browse and enjoy the effect of the sun shining through the stained-glass doors. The multicolored light seemed to burnish every surface, and she wondered again who had arranged it all. God made the sun strong enough to flow through the colored glass, but a human hand had arranged all the beautiful things to pick up the lights.

"There you are again."

Gayle looked up and saw the cleaning woman shaking her duster at her. The woman looked even smaller than she had yesterday. "I had another appointment with Mr. Langdon. Do be careful up there!"

The woman snorted. "I do this one every Tuesday." She flicked the duster at one of the gilded cherubs. "These angels don't dust themselves."

"It doesn't look very safe," Gayle said, "with the ladder so close to the edge of the balcony."

"Those chandeliers over the stairs are worse," Ernie said. "I say a prayer before I climb up there, every time."

Gayle studied the gleaming chandeliers. Bits of the rainbow light caught on the ends of the prism baubles, sparking flashes of color.

"That does look worse. Does Mr. Starek know you do such dangerous work?"

"Why would he? The Emperor has better things to do than worry about the housekeeping staff." Ernie stretched out to swipe at the other angel. "Unless you want to give me a hand, go away. I've got work to do."

Gayle shook her head. "I'm not crazy about heights, and that's very high and not very stable."

The woman shrugged. "Then go away."

THREE

A lean man with a fringe of white hair slouched in the doorway of the rehearsal hall, in conversation with Mr. Bennet. He straightened as she approached and held out his hand. "So, you're the lady organist." Accompanied with a warm smile, the words didn't feel like derision. "I'm Herb Wilkes, chief projectionist."

Frank Bennet wasn't as friendly. "It's about time. Did you find Langdon and get your paperwork done?"

"I didn't find him," Gayle said, "but Miss Fisher helped me. I got the paperwork signed, and everything's in order. I'm ready to start."

"I'd like to know where he is." Bennet ran a finger over his mustache. "Has anyone gone to his home to look for him?"

"I'm afraid I don't know." Gayle didn't want to remind him that she was just the brand-new second organist. The lady organist. "You could ask Miss Fisher."

He remained silent for a few seconds, staring through narrowed eyes at the blank screen before standing. "Let's get going on this before the orchestra arrives. *Bluff* starts on Friday, and you'll play the matinee through the weekend. You'll have Monday and Tuesday off. The score doesn't match up with the film, so you'll have to improvise. Can you do that?"

"I think so," Gayle said. "How long is the film?"

"Just an hour. No special effects. You'll sit in on the rehearsal today, just to see how it's done, but don't worry about matching Jesse or the orchestra when you do the matinees." The music director pulled a chair next to the organ bench and sat down. "Going forward, you'll learn the full orchestration for each film, in case you ever need to fill in for Jesse, but we won't start with this one. You ready, Herb?"

Gayle sat at the organ, uncomfortably close to Bennet. She could feel his tension. Was he regretting hiring her? He went through the score with her, pointing out the errors, and then pushed his chair back. "The orchestra's getting set up in the larger hall. Go ahead over there now. I'm going to see if I can find Langdon, and then I'll join you."

Maybe he wanted to find Langdon and complain about her. Gayle rose from the bench, trying to look confident and calm.

He stopped in the doorway. "You have something suitable to wear?"

"Suitable?"

He flicked a hand toward her suit. "Not that. Something formal, even for the matinees."

"Yes," Gayle said. "I'll find something."

"Good. And if you see Langdon, tell him I'm looking for him."

―――

JOHN SET the receiver back in its cradle and frowned at it. According to the landlady at Langdon's boarding house, he'd moved out three months ago.

He dialed the assistant manager's office and started talking as soon as she answered. "Are you sure Langdon didn't say anything at all about moving? Nothing?"

"No, sir. I didn't know he'd moved."

"And he hasn't shown up today." John drummed his fingers on his desk. He opened his mouth to question her further, but a shrill scream made him drop the receiver. He left it dangling as he ran to the doorway.

The sound broke off and started again, and then again, as he raced toward the lobby. One of the cleaning women stood in the middle of the hallway, fists clenched, screaming like a siren, taking breaths to gulp in air and then screaming again.

John grasped her elbow and turned her to face him. "What's the matter?"

The woman jerked away and pointed into the lobby, her whole arm quivering. "Ernie." She took a deep, shaky breath, and John hurried forward, afraid the next scream would permanently damage his hearing.

A dozen people hovered in doorways and on the edges of the lobby, unwilling to approach the small, crumpled body. Even with her face turned away from him, it was unmistakably Ernie. If there was blood, it was absorbed into the pattern of the carpet.

"Telephone the hospital. Get an ambulance!" he shouted. "Miss Fisher!"

One of the ushers muttered something about it being too late for that, and John spun to glare at him. "Get a blanket. Something to cover her."

The man disappeared, and John squatted next to the body. It was a body; he had no doubt. There was something very lifeless about poor Ernie. A complete absence of life.

John looked up. She must have fallen, to be so…crumpled. A ladder tilted sideways against the balcony. Had she been climbing that?

"Oh, no!"

John turned at the exclamation and saw Gayle running

toward him. Even in the moment, he was obscurely pleased that she was running toward them and not hanging back like the others.

"I knew she was going to fall! I warned her!" She reached out and touched Ernie's head—something John hadn't wanted to do. "Poor Ernie."

She turned to glare at him. "This is all your fault! She should never have been on that ladder so close to the edge of the balcony."

"No, she shouldn't, but I didn't tell her to do that." Stung, John looked around for the screaming girl. "I would have stopped her, if I'd known."

The girl was nowhere to be seen—or heard—but one of the ushers took a short step toward him.

"She did it all the time, sir. It's how she reached those angels, to dust them."

Gayle nodded. "I talked to her about it this morning. She said she dusts the cherubs on Tuesdays, and she said the chandeliers over the stairs were even more dangerous."

Everyone turned to look at the chandeliers. John felt sick. "How did she do that? I thought they were lowered by pulleys for cleaning."

"Well, apparently, she didn't know that," Gayle snapped.

"Yes, she did." A young girl—another cleaning woman, according to her chambray dress and apron—said. "She did know that, sir, but she didn't get on with Mr. Rogg. The maintenance man," she clarified. "She never called him unless she had to. Besides, he said the chandeliers only needed to be cleaned once a month, and she didn't think that was enough." The girl wrapped her arms around her stomach and wailed. "She liked everything so clean!"

To John's relief, Gayle stood and put an arm around the girl's heaving shoulders. "Come on. Let's find you a cup of tea with plenty of sugar in it. You'll feel better then."

John watched them go. He could use a cup of tea. If he were a drinking man, he'd want something even stronger.

He accepted the blanket from the usher, who stood as far away as possible, and told everyone to go away. He covered up the dead woman and stood, helpless and horrified at his responsibility for Ernie's death. He should have known, or someone should have told him, so he could have stopped her. This wasn't an accident. It was his fault. His negligence, and it wasn't anything he could fix, because it was too late. Ernie was dead.

NO ONE ACTUALLY SAID, "The show must go on," but Gayle knew it had to happen. As tragic and important as Ernie's death might be, the movie-going public still expected their entertainment. They didn't know Ernie or care about her.

She dragged her attention back to Jesse's lecture, wishing she could go home instead of staying to observe his performance.

"The important thing is the film," Jesse said. "The organist is there to accompany the film, not draw attention to herself—or himself, as the case may be."

They played solo pieces, too, Gayle thought, but people tended to move around during those songs. It was almost background music as people were seated and preparing to watch the show. Then they played introductions for the various acts, and sometimes accompaniment, and always music at the end to close the show. She didn't argue with him.

"The organ is directly in front of the screen," he continued, "so it's hard to not be a distraction. Black and white, or gray, clothing would be appropriate. The orchestra usually wears black and white." He adjusted his bow tie. "In fact, the women wear all black. You could wear dark gray, if you like, but it's best to stay with modest and inconspicuous garments."

"Mr. Bennet said it should be formal."

"Certainly." Jesse adjusted his bowtie. "Formal. As you can see." He swept a hand down the length of his impeccably tailored body. "Simple and formal."

Easy for him to say. Men's formal wear was always black and white. It all looked the same.

"I'm sure you can find something less…conspicuous." Jesse surveyed her Nile green dress with undisguised distaste before pushing back his cuff and checking his watch. "I need to talk to Wilkes before I go on. You'd better take your seat, so you get a good view of the whole thing. You can watch the matinee tomorrow. I'll be present for your matinee on Friday, of course."

Gayle wished he wouldn't. She was already nervous, and his lecture had made it worse. She didn't have a black dress, and she was pretty sure Dot didn't, either. The idea of borrowing a dress from her mother for her debut performance was depressing. This wasn't nearly as glamorous a job as she had expected.

GAYLE WIGGLED, enjoying the plush seat, reveling in the pleasure of sitting in an elegant box with the best view in the house. She'd dressed up for the occasion, too. She liked her green dress, and she'd planned to wear it while performing. Was it really too conspicuous? The back was cut conservatively, but the dress was sleeveless, and its bateau neckline was trimmed with metal sequins that glittered in the brilliant light of the chandeliers. Her father had raised his brows but not voiced an objection, so it couldn't be too immodest. A darker green sash wrapped just below her waist and streamed down one side of the ankle-length skirt. She wasn't even wearing any jewelry, unless one counted the artificial diamonds in the buckle of the little velvet cap. Would she really be a distraction? She felt pretty and fashionable, but not at all like a flapper. It was a stylish outfit. Too bad she couldn't wear it for work.

Gayle flopped back into the chair. She'd have to get a formal black dress. It would take a bite out of her savings account, but Jesse was right—the three women in the orchestra were dressed in severe black. She might be able to dye her brown organ shoes. A bit of black dye would hide the scuffs, too.

A hush swept across the auditorium as twilight spread across the ceiling, revealing a Moorish skyline of minarets and mosques. The pink and deep purple clouds of sunset drifted over the darkening cerulean sky. As the clouds were swallowed up in the blue darkness, stars appeared, flickering in and out against the artificial night. The audience hummed with anticipation. Gayle, too, waited for the opening chords of the riser music and watched, thrilled, as the Mighty Wurlitzer rose, glowing, from its tomb.

The music swelled into the theater as the organist made his dramatic entrance. The light of the console reflected against Jesse's satin lapels and stark white shirtfront, while the spotlight illuminated his pomaded hair. He sat upright and important on the bench, elbows bent, tails swept out behind him.

The man was a performer. He emoted his way through four songs, rocking in time with the music. Four songs, and Bennet hadn't given her any guidance. Was she supposed to play four songs for the matinee?

The Eastman School of Music's performance style was a little more refined than Jesse's, or at least less dramatic. Gayle hadn't thought much about having a personal style. The film dictated the style, didn't it? A comedy would be different from a tragedy. The concert part of the program would be her own, though. She'd have to ask Mr. Bennet about that, too.

Jesse stood up and bowed three times—toward each side

of the theater and straight ahead—and flourished his arm toward the organ. He then sat on the bench, waved in farewell, and sank out of sight. That hadn't been covered at Eastman, either. Gayle sighed.

The curtains swept open to reveal a stylized set with an orchestra of twenty women, all stylishly bobbed, with red lipstick and heavy makeup. Gayle was a little shocked by the stockinged legs displayed by the violinists seated in the front row. The black and white sleeveless dresses didn't quite cover their knees. It must be very entertaining for the musicians in the pit.

Their first song was nearly ten minutes long, and Gayle's judgmental attitude shifted to awe. After a few minutes of beautiful light music on violins and harps, they had set those down and picked up accordions. Soon, they traded those for a variety of brass instruments, and then they sang while playing banjos before returning to the violins. By the time they concluded their program and stood for their bow, Gayle was exhausted on their behalf. She could play the piano and the organ. The Ingenues might be a traveling band instead of a fine orchestra, but they were real musicians.

"Hello, Chicago!" The man striding onto the stage was nearly as round as he was tall, with a red and white striped coat straining across his belly. His unexpectedly deep voice rang through the auditorium without aid of a microphone. "Thanks for inviting us to your windy city. My name is Clive Zech—don't forget it! You'll see it in lights someday."

"See it in lights?"

Gayle searched the audience, trying to locate the source of the strident voice. A woman emerged from the darkness, stalking up the left aisle, hands on her hips.

"The day your name is in lights is the day I'll eat my hat."

"That's probably better than anything else you cook."

"Well, you don't appear to be missing any meals!"

The audience, in the mood to be entertained, laughed.

Gayle enjoyed the patter and the song and dance that followed. The vaudeville acts would be a break in her part of the program, between the opening concert and the film. Hopefully, they'd all be this entertaining and not as educational as Dot said they might be.

"Please, Lord, help me do this." Gayle muttered the last-minute prayer under her breath as she scanned the Mighty Wurlitzer's complicated console. She knew every tab and stop, and she'd already adjusted the bench so she could operate the pedalboard comfortably. She could do this. She closed her eyes, breathed deeply, and sent another prayer heavenward before stretching out her hands and launching into the riser music.

On that cue, the conductor set the lift in motion. This was it—her debut. Gayle's heart seemed to thump as loudly as the music. Her family was in the audience. Lillian would be sitting with them, probably holding one of Ruth's girls on her lap. And three thousand strangers.

She hadn't expected the warmth of the spotlight or its distracting reflection on the organ's glossy red surface. Three thousand people. Gayle drew a shaky breath and pulled her focus back to the music. She'd seize this opportunity with both hands. The humorous pun allayed her nervousness. Both hands would, indeed, be needed for her success.

The three-hour show went fast, but she kept up, through the vaudeville acts, the Ingenues and the film. Finally, the audience rose and gathered their belongings. Gayle continued playing until the theater was empty and then flipped the switch to lower the organ.

When the organ bumped gently on the basement floor, Gayle twisted her neck, stretching the tense muscles. She'd need to start taking naps in the afternoon, especially when she started doing the evening shows.

"Miss Wells."

At the sound of Mr. Bennet's voice, Gayle hastily slid from the bench and exited the organ room. She smiled brightly, confident in her performance. "How did I do?"

"You did fine, but what's this?" He flicked a hand toward her dress. "You said you had formal wear. This looks like something you borrowed from your grandmother."

Her mother, actually. Gayle glanced down at the gray rayon. "I'm sorry. I thought it was appropriate. I bought some new dresses, but they're all bright colors. I didn't think to get a black dress."

"Why on earth would you wear black?"

His impatience—and disgust?—disconcerted her. "All the other women are in black. The women in the orchestra."

"You—" Bennet pointed a finger at her. "You are not a member of the orchestra. You are the organist. A celebrity, like an actress. You should wear colors and fashionable clothes. I would think, with your fancy education, that you would be better prepared."

"But…" It would be childish to implicate Jesse.

"Take your lead from Jesse."

Gayle bit down on her tongue. Hard.

"Jesse is a star," Bennet said. "He dresses in a formal tuxedo. People expect him to look fashionable, like an actor. The organist is a performer, not just a musician."

"I'll wear something better tomorrow."

"I want to see some jewelry and more makeup, too. The Empire isn't some backwoods theater catering to country hicks. We have a reputation to uphold. I expect better tomorrow."

He spun and stalked away, leaving Gayle breathless and sick. She returned to the organ room for her music and carried it, fuming, to the musicians' locker room.

Why would Jesse want to undermine her? Was it some kind of joke or prank? He couldn't possibly see her as a threat. Still, Mr. Bennet was right. She should have known better. She'd never seen a female theater organist perform, but she knew that organists were often celebrities. Jesse was vain and conceited. Maybe he was afraid she'd be competition in the eyes of the public. She would be a novelty, after all. She might gain more attention than him.

A squeaking sound in her jaw made Gayle realize she'd switched from biting her tongue to grinding her teeth. So much for union brotherhood. She was obviously on her own here, and because of Jesse, she'd already annoyed her boss. Her mother would claim it was because she was a woman, but Gayle thought it was just because Jesse was an arrogant…

She stopped, rejecting the various epithets that occurred to her. She'd confront him, though, even if she had to do it with Christian kindness. The two weren't incompatible—at least, in theory.

She found him where she'd expected—sprawled on a sofa in the musicians' lounge, smoking and reading a newspaper. He smirked, and her ire rose again.

"Why did you tell me to dress inconspicuously? Mr. Bennet said I should wear something more fashionable and…showy."

"But all the other women are in black." Jesse feigned astonishment. "I assumed that was the standard dress for the female theater musicians. I wear black and white—the same thing as the men in the orchestra."

But he was a man, and they all wore black and white. Gayle narrowed her eyes at him.

"Sorry." He shrugged. "I didn't know. I've never seen a girl organist before. If Bennet wants you in something else, do what he says. He's the boss." He shook out his newspaper and propped his feet on the table.

She shook her head. "I think you must have known. He said organists are different. He wants us to dress like celebrities."

"Ah. Good to know." Jesse nodded and returned to his newspaper. "You went to college for this. Didn't they teach you how to perform there?"

HER MOTHER CAUGHT her in an embrace when she joined them in the lobby. "Wonderful, dear. I am so proud of you!"

"You did very well." Her father beamed, his white hair catching the colorful light in a golden halo. "I enjoyed the show, too. The movie was a bit over-dramatic for my taste, but the vaudeville act was entertaining, and the music was good. That all-girl band—Ingenues—was impressive. Such talent, to be able to play all those instruments." He reached over to take his wife's hand and tuck it inside his elbow. "I understand your mother is roasting a chicken for dinner tonight, so try to be home soon." He looked around the lobby, his brows knit. "I do worry about you still. Be careful."

She reached up to kiss his cheek. "I will."

"I saw a man from the Empire a while ago, at church. He came in on a weekday and asked if I would take his confession."

"He thought you were Catholic?" Gayle asked.

Her father shrugged. "I don't think he knew much about it. He said he'd 'got religion' and needed to confess all his sins. I told him he could take his confession directly to Jesus, but he didn't like that answer."

"How do you know he was from the Empire?" His wife asked.

"He told me. And, well…I didn't take his confession, but I

suppose I should respect his confidences and not share anything else."

Dot rolled her eyes. "Discretion, just when you've got us panting with curiosity."

"I'm sorry," he said. "I shouldn't have said anything at all."

"Well, I'm perfectly safe here, especially in the afternoons," Gayle said. "And according to Miss Fisher, a group of musicians go together to the streetcar stop after the evening shows, so you don't have to worry."

Her mother grinned. "Yes, he does have to worry. It's his job. And theater people don't have the best reputation, you know."

"I didn't say that," her husband objected.

"You were thinking it." Gayle and Dot spoke simultaneously, and they all laughed.

"Hopefully, I'll save enough money to get my own car by winter," Gayle said. "Then I won't have to take the streetcar anymore."

He opened his mouth to respond, but her mother interceded. "We need to go. We'll see you soon, dear. And…do be careful, please."

FOUR

Lillian couldn't afford this car. Gayle knew exactly how much the Special Six cost—more than she could afford if she worked seven days a week for ten years.

"Ducky, isn't it?" Lillian stroked the glossy wood of the dashboard. "Willie lent it to me for a few days."

Gayle leaned back against the cream upholstery, wondering if virtue was really worth the reward. Her friend's life was so much more glamorous than her own. "He must really be in love. Has he ever seen you drive?"

Lillian sent her a glare reminiscent of their childhood quarrels. "I am an excellent driver. I can't be responsible for all the other drivers on the road, though. Every accident I've ever had was someone else's fault."

The wind caught Gayle's hat, and she clutched at it, laughing. "It's a real sockdolager of a car, Lil. Do try not to break it."

"Maybe you'd rather take the streetcar?" Lillian sniffed. "If you're that afraid of my driving, we could even walk."

"No, I was just teasing you. I'm sorry. You're a fine driver." Gayle regretted the words as soon as they came out. She hadn't meant to hurt or offend Lillian by her joking comments, and she was quite certain Lillian knew that. She really was a terrible driver, so that part was an outright lie.

She sighed. She was always feeling guilty and apologizing to Lillian for one thing or another, and she couldn't seem to break herself of the habit. Every so often, she wondered if her friend took advantage of her circumstances. Most of the time, Lillian was so hard-boiled that Gayle forgot her tragic past—until Lillian did or said something to remind her.

"We really don't have time, anyhow." The car jerked forward as Lillian pressed on the accelerator. "Willie's mother made a big stink, and now we have to get married in a church instead of somewhere fun. She wants the whole shebang. White dress, veil, bridesmaids—you're all I've got, so that would be you—flowers and music. She'll pay for it, but I told her I'd be doing the planning. She showed me a photograph of herself at Cornelia Vanderbilt's wedding, as if I'd be impressed by their social connections." She scoffed and looked over her shoulder before turning onto the main street. "Did you ever see Cornelia Vanderbilt's wedding dress?"

"No, I don't think I have." Gayle grasped the dashboard. "There's a streetcar to your left."

Lillian swerved to the right. "Well, it's very respectable. Long sleeves, long skirt, long veil, and a huge bouquet of flowers. Her bridesmaids were even worse. Ugly hats, too, and their bouquets looked like they were carrying shrubbery."

Gayle laughed at her friend's candor. "I'd rather not wear an ugly hat. I need a few new dresses for work, though, so maybe one of those will work for the wedding. You know I'm saving money for a car. I can't afford to buy something I'll never wear again."

"Let Mrs. Fanshaw buy your dress." Lillian grunted as the roadster jolted over a hole. "I need to order my dress today, though, because I'm pretty sure I can't find what I want at Marshall Fields."

"Is there time for that?" Gayle asked.

"Mrs. Fanshaw says any dressmaker will work double time for her. We'll see about that. I've heard of a spiffy place on Broad Street. They don't make Cornelia Vanderbilt dresses." Lillian pushed on the horn to warn a pedestrian of her approach. "Willie is no society toff, either, but his mother keeps hoping he'll change."

"Hope springs eternal in the human breast," Gayle murmured. Willie would only become respectable by the grace of God. A miracle. She hadn't given up on Lillian, so she understood his mother's feelings.

"So, anyhow, I need you to do the music."

Gayle laughed. "How can I do the music and be a bridesmaid, too?"

"You'll figure it out. A processional and a couple songs and the ending music." Lillian waved a hand dismissively.

"You want me to walk down the aisle and play the organ at the same time? Can you please keep both hands on the steering wheel?"

"Oh." Lillian screwed up her face in thought.

"We can talk about it later," Gayle said, hoping to keep her friend focused on the road, "and I'm sure we'll come up with something doable. I've played for plenty of weddings at our church."

"Good. And now you're playing for money at the Empire, thanks to me!"

Gayle wondered how long she'd have to be eternally grateful to Lillian. "It's going pretty well. Things are a bit confused right now because Mr. Langdon's disappeared. The assistant manager isn't as easy-going as he is."

Lillian stomped on the brake and turned to face her. "Disappeared?"

Gayle glanced at an approaching car. It slowed and then went around them. "Yes. Can we get out of the street?"

"What happened to him?"

"No one knows. There are all sorts of rumors, of course. A couple people think the mob got him. One of the men in the orchestra swears he was running from the prohibition agents, and one of the cleaning women claims she saw him being abducted and shoved in the back of a van. Most people think he ran off with one of the girls from the last vaudeville troupe."

Lillian had that concentrated squint again. "He's not the type to take off with tomatoes. I wonder if he had to run."

"Run? Why?"

Lillian drummed her fingernails on the steering wheel. "He's not as lily-white as he pretends to be. How do you think I got you the job?"

"What do you mean?" Gayle asked. "Can we move the car, please?"

Lillian started forward again. The car lurched and stopped. She muttered under her breath and started it again. "He's just not what you think he is. He's got a past, and it might be catching up to him."

Gayle rolled her eyes. When they were children, Lillian had wanted to be an actress, and she'd never outgrown her penchant for theatrics. Gayle didn't have time for play-acting today.

"What kind of wedding dress do you want?"

"What about Frank Bennet?" Lillian demanded. "Is he still there?"

"Yes, and he's more upset than anyone about Mr. Langdon. I hadn't realized they were friends."

Lillian snorted. "Oh, yeah. They worked together in New York."

"That would explain it, then," Gayle said. "I hope he comes back soon, but I'm afraid he might not have a job to come back to. Mr. Starek is annoyed, and the assistant—Miss Fisher—is doing fine without him. I think she's hoping to get the job."

"A woman theater manager? That'll be the day." Lillian turned the car into a parking spot. "See? No accidents and no lectures from traffic police. I'm an excellent driver, or Willie wouldn't trust me with his precious car."

"SILVER? INSTEAD OF WHITE?" Gayle wondered what Mrs. Fanshaw would think of that. If Willie's mother hoped for long sleeves and a long skirt, she shouldn't have let Lillian go shopping without her. Still, it was Lillian's wedding, and Gayle wanted her friend to be happy. It was just a dress.

"It's really white, underneath," the saleswoman said. "The cloth of silver and beading are the outer layer."

"Don't say anything else," Lillian called from behind the screen. "I want it to be a surprise!"

"Of course." The saleswoman pressed a finger to her lips and smiled at Gayle. "You will be pleased. Will you want a similar dress?"

"I'm pretty sure not," Gayle muttered. Louder, she said, "No, thank you."

"You need a new dress," Lillian said. "Get it here, so we can move on to flowers."

Gayle wanted to throttle Lillian. The Blue Bodice was the most expensive shop in Chicago. She couldn't afford even the simplest dress here, and she wasn't going to let Mrs. Fanshaw buy one for her. "I have something else in mind, Lillian." She hoped she sounded pleasant, even through gritted teeth. "Come out and show me your dress!"

With a flourish, Lillian emerged from the dressing area and spun in a circle.

Gayle blinked.

"It's so lovely on you," the saleswoman gushed. "You will set a fashion for all the brides this year!"

Gayle sincerely hoped not. Lillian's dress was the epitome

of flapper fashion, with silvery beads shimmering with her every movement. It might cover her knees when she stood still, but as she admired herself in the mirror dancing the Charleston and kicking her heels, her long legs were on full display.

"Will that even stay up?" Gayle asked. "It looks like it might slide off your shoulders. There's no back at all."

Lillian stopped dancing and tugged on the pearl clasp on her shoulder. "It should be all right."

"It will stay in place." The saleswoman seemed offended. "Our dresses are cut to fit perfectly."

Lillian hunched forward. The dress sagged forward but didn't fall off. "It's fine. Don't be such a wet blanket. I want a fringed thing around my face. Not a hat." She fluttered her fingers alongside her head and the saleswoman nodded.

"The fascinator. Excellent choice. But with a veil?"

"No veil," Lillian said.

"Well…" Gayle tipped her head and considered the dress. "If you're getting married in a church, you might want a big veil to cover your back and shoulders. And maybe wrap it around your legs, too."

Lillian's laughter bubbled out like a child's, disarming Gayle and confusing the saleswoman. She threw her arms around Gayle and laughed more. "I will look like an Egyptian mummy, and I shall emerge like a butterfly from its cocoon!"

"Not while you are standing at the altar, I hope."

"Mrs. Fanshaw can buy me a veil," Lillian conceded, "but I don't know if I'll wear it."

"It would be a sin to cover up such a lovely gown," the saleswoman said, "and that would not do in a church."

Gayle ignored her. "I can get everything I need at Marshall Fields. You can probably find stockings and shoes and anything else you want there, too. I need to be back at the theater for rehearsal at two."

"Oh, you career women don't know how to have a good time." Lillian walked around the screen to change back to her day clothes. "No shopping trips with long lunches!"

"I can't be late," Gayle said. "I have a feeling Mr. Bennet would fire me if he got an excuse."

"Why on earth would he?" Lillian stuck her head out, scowling. "He's lucky to have you."

Gayle bit her lip. "I don't know. He doesn't seem to like me much."

"If he gives you any trouble, you just let me know," Lillian said. "I won't let him push you around."

"YOU MUST BE JOKING!" Gayle grasped Lillian's elbow and tugged backward. "Be careful. Traffic here is terrible." She shifted her packages. "I should have had these delivered."

"Don't be ridiculous. I can drop them off at your house after I take you to the theater. I haven't seen your mother in ages. And I'm not kidding. Willie and I love that song." Lillian tapped her foot and wiggled her shoulders. "'You are my favorite, my favorite thing!'" Her naturally contralto voice pitched higher than usual, she sang the words loudly, ignoring the people nearby. "'I have diamonds and roses and puppy dogs, too, but my favorite, favorite thing is you.'"

"For a wedding? In a church?"

"Why not? It's just a silly song, not sinful or anything." Lillian said. She narrowed her eyes. "Are you saying it's a sinful song?"

"No, but marriage is sacred, Lillian. You're making vows in front of God. With God. It's not a silly occasion. It's important. You should pick songs that are meaningful." She stopped, aware that her words sounded pious and judgmental. A condescending rebuke. Too late, she recognized the belligerent expression in her friend's eyes. Last time she'd seen that expression, their conversation had ended with shouts and tears. She didn't want to replay it now, on a crowded sidewalk.

"It's my wedding, and that song is meaningful to Willie and me. We danced it together, the first time we met. It's sentimental."

"I just care about you," Gayle said, "and I want you to be happy. Marriage is permanent—until death do you part. Do you really love Willie that much?"

"Yes!" Lillian shouted the response. "I do, and I know what you're thinking. We don't plan to get divorced. It's not like that."

"I didn't say that. Or think it." Another lie. Gayle had been thinking exactly that.

"Yes, you were. So will everyone else. Just because I want to wear a pretty dress and have jazzy music, and I like to go out and have a good time, everyone thinks I'm stupid." Her voice was getting louder. "Well, I don't care what anyone thinks. If you don't want to be in the wedding, just say so."

"I do!" Gayle kept her voice low, hoping Lillian would follow her example. "I'm sorry. I know you aren't stupid." Another apology.

"Just too trashy to plan a proper wedding! You probably think I should wear a long dress and have a boring ceremony with a choir singing 'The Voice that Breathed O'er Eden' and a dozen little flower girls in white dresses." She poked a painted fingernail at Gayle. "That's you, not me."

"That's not me," Gayle said. "That was Ruth's wedding, and you and I were adorable in our little white dresses."

Lillian refused to be diverted. "Mrs. Fanshaw thinks that would be just peachy. A big cathedral with all the works. She said she'd be happy to organize it for me, since I don't have a mother of my own."

"Oh, Lilly…" Gayle reached out, but her friend pulled away.

"So, I'm going to have it my own way—mine and Willie's—and if she doesn't like it, she doesn't have to come." Lillian's voice, taut and loud, drew attention. The crowd of shoppers and workers on their way to lunch stared openly. "I was counting on you to support me, not criticize everything I want."

Arguments with Lillian were always like this. She pecked and prodded until someone else threw the first punch. Then she could feel justified for indulging in a dramatic tantrum, abused and misunderstood. Gayle had never learned the trick of winning that game, and she knew this one would end just as all the others did—with Lillian in tears and Gayle apologizing for something she didn't quite understand. She just wished they didn't have an audience.

"It will all work out," she said.

"I know it will all work out!" Lillian shouted. "I don't care what anyone else thinks. You're being narrow-minded and nasty because you're jealous!"

That was a new one. Gayle opened her mouth and shut it again. She might as well let Lillian run her course. They'd discuss the music again later. It wasn't that "You Are My Favorite Thing" was a bad song. It was just silly. Too silly for a wedding. Not even Papa, who extended a remarkable amount of grace to Lillian, would approve of it.

"You're jealous!" Lillian stabbed a finger at her, and Gayle slapped it away.

She gasped as Lillian stumbled into the road, falling on her hip, and rolling backward, eyes wide and shocked.

Cars swerved around her, horns blaring, but a streetcar surged forward on its track. A woman screamed and pulled her child back, shielding his eyes from the horror to come.

Gayle dropped her packages and reached for her friend, but a burly policeman was faster. He scooped up Lillian around the waist, carrying her back to the sidewalk and dropping her on her feet. Her knees buckled, and he held her arm until she was steady.

The policeman stood between them, scowling. "I ought to charge you with assault, young lady. Or reckless endangerment, at the least."

"Me?" Gayle's squeak was lost in Lillian's indignant response.

"No, not her! Someone else pushed me. Hard. Maybe it was a kick." She looked around. "Someone must have seen him. He pushed me right into the street."

"Who did? A man? Did you see him?" The policeman pulled a small notebook from his pocket and folded it open. He continued talking while he fished out a pencil. "I didn't see a man, and I'm quite observant. I mean, there were several men, but they weren't quarreling with you as this lady was. Your friend pushed your hand away. You stumbled and fell, being much too close to the street and not paying attention to anything but your own conversation." His brogue was heavy, adding a note of censure to his comments.

"No! Someone pushed me. On my hip. I'll have a bruise."

The policeman glanced where she was pointing and hastily averted his eyes. "I didn't see any of that."

Neither had Gayle, but she knew it wasn't her slap that had sent Lillian into the path of traffic. "There were a lot of people around. We were standing, talking, and people were walking past us." Some had loitered, entertained by their quarrel.

"Someone must have seen him," Lillian insisted. She turned to their audience. "One of you witnessed it."

The crowd dispersed quickly at that, only a few older women remaining to offer advice. One claimed to have seen a suspicious man in a dark suit hanging around. Another said a hobo had done it.

The police officer, clearly not convinced, sent them off. He bent another suspicious look at Gayle before returning his attention to Lillian. "Do you want to come to the station and file an incident report, Miss?"

Lillian picked up her hat and punched it back into shape. "No, I'll take care of it myself."

The police officer shook his head. "You need to leave it to the police, Miss."

"No, I will take care of this myself." She scowled at Gayle. "Let's get to the theater."

GAYLE TRAILED AFTER HER FRIEND, dragged ruthlessly through the stained-glass doors.

"I should use the side door. I'm supposed to be starting the matinee soon, and I need to change clothes."

"You have plenty of time. I want to talk to this assistant of yours of Langdon's. Assistants always know what's going on. She knows where he is. I guarantee it."

"Over there." Gayle pointed. "It looks like there are people in there. We should wait till they're finished."

"He just pushed me in front of a streetcar!" Lillian said. "I'm not waiting!"

Could Mr. Langdon have pushed Lillian? Gayle had assumed it was an accident. Lillian had stepped back and tripped over her own feet, but it had been an odd, sideways sort of fall, and Lillian had looked startled…Gayle followed her into the office.

They didn't hear the deep voices until they stood in the doorway. Both girls stopped, astonished.

"Michael!"

Gayle's brother-in-law frowned at her. "It's Sergeant Brady here. I'm on official business."

Lillian snickered and he transferred the frown to her. He'd

been indulgent with the two little girls and sympathetic when Lillian's parents died but he'd disapproved of her for years now, personally and professionally. "And why are you here, Miss Nagle?"

For a few seconds, Gayle thought Lillian might make a flippant response, possibly calling him Mickey, but her friend stalked into the room and leaned over Miss Fisher's desk. "I want to see Hewitt Langdon. Now."

The assistant was pale, chewing on her bottom lip, clasping her hands together and darting glances between John Starek and the big policeman. "I don't know where he is." It sounded like a refrain, repeated regularly over the past week. "I don't."

"None of us do," Mr. Starek said. He nodded at Gayle. "Miss Wells. Can I help you with anything?"

Gayle wished she could sink through the floor. He must think she was the most incompetent employee ever.

"She's with me," Lillian said. "She's a witness."

"I didn't see anything," Gayle objected.

"Witness?" Michael obviously thought Lillian was being over-dramatic. "Witness to what?"

"Langdon just tried to kill me."

Miss Fisher gasped. "Mr. Langdon? When?"

"Just now. Half an hour ago," Lillian said, "and you can't tell me you don't know where he is."

The assistant shook her head, more like a dog shaking off water than a sign of negation. "I'm sure it wasn't him. It couldn't have been."

"Mr. Langdon tried to kill you?" Michael didn't quite roll his eyes, but his resigned patience had the same effect. "You're talking about the theater manager who disappeared one week ago?" He consulted his notebook. "Hasn't been seen since Tuesday, before Miss Ernst was killed."

"Was killed?" Mr. Starek asked. "That's an odd way to say

it. She fell off the ladder and over the railing. It was an accident."

"Pending further medical examination," Michael said, "a head injury indicates the possibility that she experienced a blow to the head, with a blunt instrument, previous to her fall."

"You mean someone killed her?" Lillian dropped onto the visitor chair.

"And then set it up to look like an accident," Michael said. He looked at his watch. "Two men will be along soon to examine the scene of the crime."

"It's been cleaned," Miss Fisher said, "and it's a public area. People have been walking there."

"Langdon probably did that, too," Lillian said.

"Cleaned…killed the cleaning woman? And why would he do that?" Michael asked.

"Why would anyone kill a cleaning lady?" John Starek asked.

"She knew too much," Lillian said darkly.

"Knew too much about Mr. Langdon? Is there something to know, or are you just making up stories, Miss Lillian?" Exasperated, Michael put his notebook back in his pocket.

Gayle thought Lillian might stomp her foot, but she just regarded Michael through narrowed eyes for a few seconds before returning to Miss Fisher. "You must know where he is."

"I do not." The assistant looked at Gayle. "I believe your rehearsal is starting."

Gayle squeaked. "I need to go."

Her brother-in-law put a hand on her shoulder and addressed the room in general. "Just a few more minutes. I must also inform you that after the death of Miss Ernst, we are re-examining the accidental death of Henry Glassman."

"Why?" The wail came from Miss Fisher. "Everything was going so well!"

They all stared at her. She turned pink and started fussing

with the telephone cord. "I mean, at the theater. I can't imagine why anyone here would kill either of them."

Michael raised his brows. "We will, naturally, be making inquiries to see if they were associated outside the theater."

They all knew he didn't believe it. If Mr. Glassman had been murdered—shoved in front of a streetcar, like Lillian—it had to be connected to the Empire.

FIVE

Gayle tried not to fidget. Lillian's idea of appropriate makeup probably aligned with Mr. Bennet's, and she'd already gotten in trouble for not dressing the part. She knew the spotlights would make her look shiny without the powder Lillian had puffed all over her face. She just didn't like it.

"I feel silly." Gayle scratched her eyebrow with a fingernail. "I don't even put on this much makeup in the evenings."

Lillian snatched the mirror from her hand. "You look nifty." She picked up a kohl stick and sharpened it on an emery board. "The cat's meow."

"Cat's meow?"

Lillian pulled on the side of Gayle's eyelid and drew a line. "Hold still."

"Ouch!"

Lillian ignored her complaint. "You need to know how to do it yourself, so pay attention. After you put the eyeliner on, you smear it upward and under your eyes, too." She smeared.

"Can I see the mirror? I can't tell what you're doing."

"In a minute." Lillian rubbed the mascara brush in its

pan. "Shut your eyes like this." She demonstrated, and Gayle did her best to copy the expression.

Gayle had worn mascara, of course, in New York. She'd even worn powder and rouge and lipstick. The kohl was new, though, and she'd seen enough films to dread the result. Her father would be horrified. "Are you sure I need all of this?"

"Yes," Lillian said firmly. "And a bit of rouge, right here." She applied it liberally and held up the cake. "Pompeian Bloom. It's new." She wrinkled her nose. "It's not exactly the right skin tone. My skin is lighter than yours, and I bought the oriental tint. You'll have to buy some for yourself, anyhow. They have a good cosmetic counter at Marshall Fields. We could go back there after the show today."

"Are you coming to the show?"

"Wouldn't miss it. You'll be a bigger sheba than Agnes Ayres on the screen." Lillian leaned back and studied her with apparent satisfaction. "I have an outline card for your lips. It's easier than me doing it."

"A sheba?" Gayle sat upright. "My father would disown me! I'm not the sheba type. I don't want to be the sheba type. Give me that mirror."

"No, do the lips first," Lillian pleaded. She pushed the mirror further away. "You can do them yourself. Just trace through the opening."

"I can do my lips without that."

"I've seen you do your lips," Lillian said. "It's not anywhere close to a bow."

"I don't want a bow." Gayle reached for the mirror, but Lillian grabbed it up.

"Lips first."

"Fine, but I can't do it without the mirror."

"Then I'll do it." Lillian swiveled up the red lipstick and leaned forward. "Pull the corners of your lips back. No, don't open your mouth."

Gayle complied, and as soon as Lillian finished, she scrambled for the mirror. The face staring back at her was ridiculous in the bright morning light. She stood up and headed for the bathroom. "I look like I'm sick, with a fever and dark circles under my eyes!"

Lillian trailed after her. "It's the rouge. It's the wrong shade." She rolled her eyes as Gayle turned on the faucet. "You'll need cold cream. Water won't take that off."

Gayle opened a cabinet and rummaged for her mother's cold cream. "It's all of it, Lillian, including the eye shadow. You did a great job, but I'm not you, and I'm not going out dancing."

"But you said you had to look like an actress!"

Gayle dabbed cream around her eyes. "More like Mary Pickford than Theda Bara, please. Do you have time to help me with it again?"

"Yes." Lillian dragged out the word with mock impatience. "And we can do Mary Pickford. She's not really very exciting, though. How about Lillian Gish?"

"Better than Theda Bera. But I don't want to be a sheba or a vamp or even a flapper. I may have to dress up and act like an actress, but I'm going to be a respectable one."

THE SHOW HAD GONE WELL. She'd even managed to stand up and bow to the audience after her solo, smiling and pretending to be Mary Pickford, wishing she could see Lillian's reaction. She was giggling as she sat down again and started the transition piece, fading out as Clive Zech strolled onto the stage. This was what she'd expected from her new career. It was supposed to be fun.

Mr. Bennet wasn't waiting for her when she stepped from the organ room, so her performance and appearance must have been acceptable. Gayle peeked in the lounge on her way to the dressing room. Jesse stood near the window in conversation with a man in a blue suit. As if sensing her presence, he looked over and saw her. He beckoned, and Gayle entered the room with a sigh. She had a feeling Jesse wasn't going to commend her for a great performance.

"Miss Wells. May I introduce Mr. Marty Shores? Marty, this is Miss Gayle Wells."

The man was no taller than Gayle but twice her weight, with a pink complexion and a head of improbably thick sandy hair. She held out her hand, but instead of shaking it, he clasped it in both of his own and bowed.

"Ah, the lovely lady organist who has been playing the matinee shows."

She pulled her hand back and nodded. "Yes, the matinees and some of the evening shows."

Jesse tapped a cigarette out of his case. "You won't need to do those anymore. Marty's taking those on, and some of the matinees."

Gayle tucked a strand of hair behind her ear, taking time to compose herself before replying. "A third organist? Is there enough work for three of us?"

The men exchanged glances. Jesse smoothed his mustache with one manicured finger. "It will give you more time off, to go out dancing with your young man or do whatever it is you ladies do at home in the evenings."

In other words, Jesse wanted a man for the job. A man less attractive than himself, too, who would not steal his limelight.

As if reading her mind, Jesse held up a hand. "Mr. Bennet hired him yesterday. Your job is safe. It takes more than two organists, with two or more shows, seven days a week."

"I thought we were doing fine." Her chest was tight, and it was hard to keep her voice even.

Jesse shook his head. "You don't want to work on Sundays, so that leaves me to do both shows every Sunday. No breaks! What if I want to go to church?"

Ha. Gayle opened her mouth to reply, but before she

could respond, Jesse rushed on. "Mr. Bennet hired him. It's his decision."

Gayle spun on her heel and left them. She shut her ears to their chuckles—if there were any—and strode to the music director's office. This was unacceptable.

She knocked and waited, but no one answered. Gayle turned in a circle, not meeting the eyes of the other people in the hallway. Maybe he wasn't at the theater today. Maybe he was hiding from her. Weasel.

"If you're looking for Bennet, he's backstage." The maintenance man didn't slow as he walked past, bald head shining in the overhead light. Rogg seemed to be everywhere, never saying much, but she didn't think he missed much, either.

She wasn't going to chase Mr. Bennet backstage and confront him in front of an interested audience. Gayle sat on a nearby chair, tapping her foot on the carpet. She'd been given a job, and now it was being taken from her for no good reason. Her union representative was no help. Mr. Langdon was Frank Bennet's boss, but Langdon was gone. Did Miss Fisher have enough authority to help her? Wouldn't another woman see the injustice of it? Could she approach John Starek about this? He seemed like a fair man, not a misogynist like Bennet and Jesse.

The door opened. "Are you looking for me?"

Bennet's exaggerated patience set her teeth on edge. He'd expected her, and that made her even more mad. Losing control now would only confirm the music director's low opinion of her. Gayle took a deep breath and composed herself.

"Can I speak to you alone?"

He turned, and she followed him into the office, stopping short at the sight of two men in armchairs near the fireplace.

"You know Art Hadley and Chester Klee, I believe. Trumpet and drums. Gentlemen, Miss Wells needs my attention for a while. If you wouldn't mind…" He gestured toward the door, and they rose and strolled out, obnoxious smirks on their faces.

Her irritation gave her courage. "I met Mr. Shores just now, and he says he's playing the evening shows."

"Very good organist," Bennet said. "We're lucky to get him. He was the chief organist at the Roxy, but it burned down last week, so he's available."

"You said I would be doing one or two evening shows every week." She kept both feet on the floor. She already sounded like a petulant child. Stomping her foot would make it worse.

Bennet shrugged. "We'll see. Shores has a family to support. Half a dozen kids to feed."

And it would be selfish of her to take food from the mouths of hungry children. Deflated, Gayle turned away. This was her job, and she mattered, too. She'd been here first. If Shores was so good, he could find a job somewhere else.

THE DOOR to the assistant manager's office was open. Gayle rapped on the doorframe. "Hello?"

Miss Fisher looked up with a jerk, knocking her pen onto the floor. Not a great start.

"Do you have a minute?" Gayle asked.

"Only a minute."

The woman's words were brisk, but her expression was… haunted. Gayle wondered at the word that had entered her mind. The woman was probably just overwhelmed with her new responsibilities. She might be facing opposition from the men at the theater, too. She'd understand Gayle's position.

"I want to talk to you about a situation I'm having," Gayle said, "with Mr. Bennet. Jesse Erwin, too."

"Mr. Bennet is your supervisor. Have you talked to him directly?" The question sounded mechanical. Disinterested.

"Yes, I have," Gayle said. How could she say that the men were conspiring to get rid of her without sounding whiney? She might even be wrong. Maybe they all disliked her individually. "I understand the need for a third organist, since there are so many shows every week, but I was offered a specific schedule. I was to play most of the matinees and some of the evening shows. Now, Mr. Bennet has hired Mr. Shores, and he's giving the evening shows to him. Jesse Erwin agrees with him."

"It's their department." Miss Fisher retrieved her pen and leaned back in the chair. "I can't interfere, if they think this new organist is a better performer than you are."

Gayle scowled. "It has nothing to do with my performance. They said he should work the shows because he's a man and needs to support his family. I don't want to sound cold-hearted, but that's not fair. They said I could have the evenings off to go dancing with my young man and do things at home."

Miss Fisher raised her brows. "They said that? Just like that?"

Gayle tried to remember the conversation. "I think those were their words. And…" she hesitated, hoping to avoid the whininess. "I think they don't like the idea of a woman organist. I think Jesse doesn't want the competition. But I'm not trying to compete!"

Miss Fisher tapped the pen on the desk. "The audiences like you because you're different."

"And because I'm a good organist," Gayle said. "I deserve this job, not because I'm a woman, but I've been here longer, and I was offered that schedule. And I'm a good organist."

"You've only been here a few weeks, just a little longer than Mr. Shores. But it does sound like you have a valid complaint. I won't have them treating you that way."

It sounded like a power point for Miss Fisher, not exactly a defense of Gayle. If the manager went in and lectured Mr.

Bennet on his behavior, things might get worse. But what had she gone to Miss Fisher for, if not for support?

"I don't want to cause trouble," she began, "and I don't want him mad at me."

Miss Fisher considered her. "This is unfortunate, Miss Wells. I will speak to them, but I have to tell you that Mr. Bennet consulted with me before hiring Mr. Shores. I approved his hire because he has an excellent reputation and years of experience. He should be a valuable asset to the theater, because he already has a following."

"But I'm just as good, and I have training, and people like me, too." Gayle hoped she sounded assertive instead of argumentative.

"When he came to see me, Mr. Bennet also expressed his concern that you don't have much experience. He said you are learning, and he's satisfied with your work so far, but you aren't quite as good as Mr. Shores."

"I am!" Gayle bit her tongue, immediately regretting the outburst. She didn't know if she was as good as Mr. Shores or not.

"I will talk to them about treating you with respect—not belittling you because you are a woman."

That should go well. Gayle didn't think that a woman lecturing men on their treatment of another woman would have a good outcome.

"If you come to one of my shows, I think you'll see that I'm a good organist," she said.

Miss Fisher looked affronted. "Of course, I've been to your shows. Three of them, I think. I will also go to see Mr. Shores's shows. I do keep a watch on what happens in the theater."

"I didn't mean it that way," Gayle said. "I'm sorry. I am sure you're doing a good job filling in for Mr. Langdon."

The woman stood. "I will talk to the men."

"Please don't." Gayle remained in her chair. "I don't want to make it worse."

"I'm in charge here, and this is a problem I need to take care of." Miss Fisher walked to the doorway, waiting for Gayle to leave. "I'm not letting things go just because they're uncomfortable or inconvenient."

Miserable, Gayle trudged back to the musicians' locker room, hoping it would be empty. Miss Fisher was about to throw kerosene on the fire, and Gayle's career would be the one left in ashes.

Was she wrong? What if Marty Shores would be better for the Empire than she was? The novelty of a woman playing the organ wasn't enough to sustain a following.

Caught up in her thoughts, she nearly tripped over the cleaning girl. The girl yelped and splashed water on the flocked wallpaper.

"I'm sorry. Let me help you with that. Do you have a dry rag?" Gayle blotted the water off the wallpaper, hoping they could prevent any damage.

"Thanks, miss. I can do that."

Focused on the work, Gayle failed to hear the footsteps approaching.

"Look at that," Jesse said. "Miss Wells doing women's work. You can do it all, can't you, Gayle? You can be a musician and a cleaning woman. Can you cook, too?"

Gayle rose, praying that God would control her tongue, stopping the blistering reaction.

He raised a hand before she could speak. "Very unkind of me, and so inappropriate. I apologize." He turned and walked away in the other direction, and Gayle was left standing, uncertain.

THE DAY STRETCHED UNBEARABLY as Gayle created the music for the new film. It had come with a sketchy cue sheet instead of a score, and rather than improvising for each showing, she wanted to write out a plan for the music ahead of time.

Jesse lounged in a chair at the other end of the rehearsal hall, smoking and making derisive sounds periodically. She wasn't certain if Miss Fisher had spoken to him or not, but his hostility was as bad as ever. He'd scoffed and said a professional organist ought to be prepared for improvisation. Gayle didn't mind improvisation on occasion, but with a dozen showings, she preferred to have a plan.

Today, he seemed to be bent on upsetting her. The Ingenues had left, and the new musical act was shorter, so the organist had to add another song. Something jazzy, Mr. Bennet said, to get the audience in the mood to enjoy the vaudeville act.

She'd spent the morning practicing "Can't Catch My Baby" while Jesse read the newspaper. When Mr. Bennet and Herb Wilkes had stopped by the rehearsal room, Jesse announced that he was playing "Can't Catch My Baby" for the extra song. Gayle would have to pick another one. She'd said nothing, just narrowed her eyes at Jesse, who smiled blandly in return.

Now, still outraged, she made notations on sheet music, wishing he would leave. He wasn't rehearsing—just sitting, lounging, and filling the air with noxious fumes. How could anyone stand to smoke cigarettes? They made her eyes water and her nose twitch.

Finally, she slammed her hands down on the keys. The music reverberated throughout the room.

"Why are you doing this? You're so critical all the time, and you undermine me with Mr. Bennet. You knew I was playing that song, and you just made it up that you were. And…" Gayle flung out a hand. "You deliberately set me up to look stupid on that first show, telling me to wear gray or black."

"Not at all. You'll catch on." He sounded as if he might pat her hand in an avuncular way. "You're doing just fine."

"Yes, I am! In spite of your attempts to sabotage me and this business of hiring another organist and giving him my evening shows!"

"Calm down." His comforting tone made it worse.

Gayle swept her papers into a pile, shoved them into her bag, and turned to leave. She stopped at the sight of Mr. Bennet, Art Hadley, and Chester Klee in the doorway.

"Is there a problem?" Bennet raised his brows.

"No, nothing at all. Miss Wells has had a stressful day." Jesse smiled benevolently. "Ernie's death, of course, and now she's having to learn to improvise for the new show."

Mr. Bennet frowned. "Do you need some time off, Miss Wells? I'm sure Mr. Shores would be glad to take over some of your shows until you feel better."

Gayle was speechless. She opened her mouth, saw the satisfaction in Jesse's face, and swallowed her defense.

"No, sir, I'm fine. I do know how to improvise, but I prefer to be prepared. And I'm not at all upset." She winced. "I mean, I am upset about Ernie's death, but it won't interfere with my work."

"Good." Bennet looked at both of them and stepped into the room. "Are you finished here? These men need to use the room for a while."

Bennet stood aside and waited for her to leave. He closed the heavy door behind her with only a small thunk. Apparently, Jesse was welcome to stay.

SIX

It had been a long show. The last vaudeville number had flopped, and Mr. Bennet had signaled to Gayle to play another song to lighten the mood before the audience started collecting their belongings to leave.

Caught off guard, she'd played a familiar piece by Bach, only to receive a blistering reprimand from Mr. Bennet. He wanted jazz, not church music. Next time, she should be prepared with something more suitable for the theater audience.

Gayle pulled her raincoat from her locker and slid into it. She wrapped an artificial silk scarf over her head and around her neck, more to protect her new hat than to stay warm, and pulled on her gloves before hoisting the strap of her portfolio over her shoulder. The bulky leather pack, left over from her school days, was oversized for sheet music, so she'd taken to carrying personal items in it also, rather than add a purse to her burden.

"Miss Wells, are you leaving already?" Mr. Bennet called from behind her as she reached the Clark Street exit.

Exhausted and upset, Gayle wished she could slip out the door and pretend she hadn't heard him. Instead, she turned.

"Yes. You might warn Mr. Shores that the vaudeville show is a problem. I don't know what happened to that girl. If she's sick, I wish I'd known ahead of time." It was a bit rude, if not disrespectful, to talk to her boss like that, but she wanted to leave. Her head hurt, and she just wanted to get home and crawl into bed.

"I'll let him know. The act was bad." He crossed his arms. "I noticed you were up in the Arabian lounge earlier. You know you're supposed to use the musicians' bathroom."

"There was a sign on the door," Gayle said. "It wasn't working." Did the man follow her around and notice which bathroom she used? Creepy.

"I see." He nodded. "I'll talk to Moe Rogg about it. We can't have the musicians wandering around the theater."

Really? Gayle's headache was spreading to her eyes. "No, sir. I hope they get it fixed quickly."

She felt his eyes on her as she slipped out the door. It was a miserable day, with layers of dark clouds blotting out any hint of afternoon sun. They hung low, spitting rain. A cold wind tried hard to penetrate her coat.

She wouldn't have wanted to drive herself in this weather. This was the kind of weather for streetcars, as long as she didn't have to wait very long. She barely caught it, in fact, and sank gratefully into a seat, regardless of the grime.

The scarf slipped down, and Gayle removed her gloves before adjusting it, winding the scarf around her neck, and tucking the ends inside her coat. She stuffed her gloves in her pockets and touched something cool and hard in the left one. She pulled out a small glass ball, iridescent even in the dim light. Gayle frowned, rolling the glowing orb in her palm. She'd seen it before. A bowl full of these marbles sat in an alcove near the Arabian lounge, but she hadn't even had her coat on when she'd been there, and she would have noticed if she'd picked one up. She hadn't even gone near the bowl.

"That's pretty," said the woman next to her. "What is it?"

"I don't know," Gayle said. "I just found it in my coat pocket."

"A gift, maybe?" The woman's round face split in a broad smile. "From a secret admirer."

It seemed unlikely that any man would give her such a gift, especially in this manner. Besides, all the men she worked with seemed to dislike her.

"Maybe," she said. "I don't know."

"There was no card?" The woman asked. "Even a secret admirer would have left a card."

Gayle pulled out her gloves and dug into her pockets. "No, nothing like that."

The woman, fascinated, was inclined to speculate, and Gayle was glad to exit at the next stop.

"I hope you find out who gave it to you, dearie!" The woman waved as Gayle stepped off the streetcar.

Gayle hastened home, disturbed by the presence of the ball. What should she do with it? She could consult her father, or try to return it to the bowl without anyone noticing, or even take it directly to Miss Fisher. Gayle winced at the thought of explaining—or being unable to explain—the situation to Miss Fisher. John Starek might be more understanding, but she couldn't go to him. That left her father.

"Papa?" She closed the door behind her, heaving a grateful sigh when the howling wind was silenced by the solid door.

"He's not here. He has that conference in Joliet this week, remember?" Her mother appeared in the kitchen doorway. "You're soaked! Get that coat off, and I'll make some hot tea. You look tired."

"I am. I have a headache," Gayle admitted, "and work was especially difficult today." She hung her dripping coat on a hook and followed her mother into the kitchen, glad to leave the troublesome ball in the pocket. Changing her mind, she returned to the hallway and took the ball from the coat pocket, dropping it into her portfolio.

"Where'd you go?" Her mother called from the kitchen. "I have some aspirin here, and then you should go change into your bathrobe and slippers. Or do you want a hot bath first?"

"Bath, please, after a cup of tea." Gayle sank onto a chair. "It was a long day. The vaudeville act—a dancing number— fell apart because one of the girls forgot the steps or something. She just stopped, and the other girl kept going. If it had been a comedy number, it would have been fine, but it was obviously a flub, so the audience was confused. Mr. Bennet ran up and told me to play another song—mad, as if it was my fault—and then he didn't like the one I played. I'm not a mind reader."

Her mother bustled around the kitchen, offering sympathetic murmurs and agreement as Gayle poured out her complaint. The interlude was soothing, and Gayle went off to her bath in a better frame of mind.

Was it possible that one of the other musicians had stolen the ball and slipped it into her pocket by mistake? Or intentionally? She didn't know why they would. Maybe, instead of her father, she should talk to Michael.

SKULKING AROUND LIKE A SPY. She'd worn her mother's gray coat and a gray scarf over her hat, hoping to fade into the gloomy, early morning weather, but maybe she'd overdone the drama. A few of Ruth and Michael's early-rising neighbors cast curious looks in her direction as they headed for the streetcars.

This neighborhood, with rutted streets laid out in tight grids, featured rows of workers cottages distinguished only by their paint colors. Ruth hoped to move to a nicer area someday, but this was convenient and affordable on Michael's salary. He'd grown up just two streets over, and his family still lived there.

Didn't Michael start work at seven? Exasperated, Gayle pulled her scarf closer and walked toward the corner. He'd have to come this direction to catch the streetcar, but she'd hoped to intercept him closer to home so they could talk.

At last, he emerged from the house, pushing the door shut behind him. Gayle hastened toward him, hoping his long strides didn't mean he was in too much of a hurry to talk to her.

He came to an abrupt stop as soon as he recognized her. "What are you doing here?"

"I need to talk to you."

He grasped her elbow and headed for the corner, pulling her along with him. "The streetcar will be here any minute. You'll have to talk on the way."

"That's not enough time! I need to tell you something."

"I can't be late for work," Michael said. "If it's so urgent, you'll have to come along on the streetcar."

It would be crowded, and Michael would stand. Gayle shook her head. "I can't. Look." She fished in her pocket and came out with the marble. "I found this in my coat pocket on the way home from work yesterday. It's part of a display…a piece of art at the Empire. I have no idea how it got there, but I was close to it yesterday."

Michael stopped, standing at a distance from his neighbors. "What do you mean, you were close to it?"

"I had to use the ladies' lounge—the public one, for guests—because the one we're supposed to use was closed. There's a bowl of these marbles there, but I didn't take any! I used the bathroom and went back to work. On my way home, I found this in my pocket."

He held out his hand, and she dropped the ball into his palm. He poked at it. "This is some kind of art? Is it valuable?"

"I would think so." The streetcar appeared in the distance, and she continued. "Mr. Bennet—my boss—knows I was up there."

"Hmm…" Michael handed the ball back to her. "Keep it for now, at home in a safe place. We're going back to the Empire today, and there'll be police all over. Maybe you'll get a chance to return it tomorrow."

"But I didn't take it," Gayle tugged on his sleeve. "How did it end up in my coat pocket?"

"I don't know. I've got to go now." He shook her off. "I'll be talking to you later."

SEVEN

The police were back, and Michael Brady wasn't in charge. He hovered near Detective Ashe, so John guessed Brady must outrank the men waiting behind them. He wondered what relationship the man had with Gayle Wells. He hadn't missed the way the police officer had stopped her with a hand on her shoulder. The other woman—Lillian?—had seemed to know him, as well.

"Miss Ernst was hit on the back of the head with a marble statue of an Egyptian cat," the detective told the officers. "It was at hand on a table forty feet down the hallway. The balcony." He consulted his notes. "If Miss Ernst didn't fall over when she was hit, she was thrown over by the assailant. There was no indication that she was conscious when she fell."

She hadn't tried to defend herself or land safely, John thought. She'd just fallen like a rag doll. Poor Ernie. She may or may not have seen her killer, but she must have known who he was. The police hadn't taken the wandering madman theory seriously after the missing statue was found on the third floor, in a cabinet in the Seraglio ballroom. A stranger—especially a madman—would have been seen climbing to the third floor or on his way down again.

"We have a list of staff members and will conduct interviews by department." The detective handed a sheaf of papers to Brady, who started distributing them to the other police officers. "We want alibis, last sightings of Ernst, Langdon and Glassman, information and rumors. You know what to do."

"Brady and I will be working with Mr. Starek and a man from his insurance company to inventory all the valuables in the theater. It's possible Miss Ernst saw something suspicious. She'd be in a position to notice missing items or people where they shouldn't be. During your interviews, ask if anyone heard her talking about that. Ask if they've noticed missing items or have heard rumors of thefts."

Ernie noticed everything, John thought. She probably knew more about what was happening at the theater than Langdon or Miss Fisher.

The police officers dispersed, flipping their notebooks open and getting directions from Michael. Ashe approached John and nodded.

"Mr. Starek. Are you and your insurance representative ready to do the inventory?"

"Yes, I have the list, and he'll be here in just a minute. You seem very organized."

"Theft seems like the most obvious motive here," Ashe said. "The housekeeper might have seen or heard something that made her suspicious. Do you think she would have tried to blackmail someone?"

John shook his head. "It seems unlike her. She was the kind of person who didn't keep secrets. She talked about everything."

"She could have stolen things, too," Ashe persisted, "and someone found out. They struggled, and she lost."

"But why would they struggle with her? Wouldn't they just turn her in?" John asked.

"People are unpredictable," the detective said, "but it

doesn't seem likely that she was a thief. Is that your insurance man?"

The search lasted four hours, and by the time they reached the lower level, John was exhausted and embarrassed. The insurance man scowled, making more notes than the police did. His stream of criticism was unfair, John thought, since he'd never even made a claim. He'd never noticed anything missing.

The police just poked around. John had no idea what they were looking for.

"This level contains most of the working areas of the theater," John said, "including offices for the music and stage departments, maintenance, and housekeeping…that kind of thing. The other side has the engineering and technical departments and the upper parts of the refrigeration and boiler rooms." He rubbed the back of his neck. "I mean, they're not really rooms—more like big areas in the basement that are two stories high. Not all the way open to this level."

"This isn't the basement?" Ashe asked. "What else is down there?"

John shrugged. "Storage. Empty office spaces. The architect who designed the Empire had a lot of grandiose ideas that fell apart under practical considerations—like money. They started things and didn't finish them."

"And that's the bottom level?"

"As far as I know." John grinned. "Every so often, someone starts spreading ghost stories. It's ridiculous, since the Empire is less than five years old, but it's the kind of place that feels like it *ought* to be haunted, if you know what I mean."

"Are there any insured items in the basement?" the insurance man asked. "I don't have anything on my list. Can we get back to this level?"

"Yes, of course. I just meant that while the rest of the theater is pretty empty at this time of day, this level is where you'll find the action. Where the staff is. There are guest areas, but they're all in that direction."

He pointed, and as if in confirmation, a crash of cymbals came from the hallway behind them, followed by loud, rollicking music. Ashe tipped his head in that direction. "I'll go check on the interviews. Brady, you can stay with them."

"Yes, sir." The police officer turned to the insurance agent. "Do you have a list of places you need to inspect? Where would you like to start?"

THESE HALLWAYS NEEDED MORE BENCHES. Tired of following the insurance agent from room to room, listening to the man's comments and watching him make notes, John fetched a chair from the housekeeping lounge and set it by Brady before getting one for himself. "Have a seat. He doesn't need either of us."

The police officer shook his head. "Ashe would appear as soon as I sat down. He's like that."

"Well, I'm sitting." John dropped onto a chair and stretched out his legs. "My grandfather was upset when we learned that Ernie's death wasn't an accident. We talked about the theft theory, but we weren't imagining anything like this." He gestured toward the thick stack of papers on the insurance agent's clipboard. "Now I have to go home and tell him I've lost quite a few of the Empire's treasures."

"At least twenty items," Brady said, "and a few damaged pieces, too. To be fair, not all of those are likely to be related to Miss Ernst's murder."

"I know. That's the problem." John tipped his chair back and brooded. It would be a shame if they had to hide all the treasures of the theater or secure them behind glass. "I'm irresponsible and foolish. Just ask that man right there."

The insurance man's sour expression indicated that he'd heard the comment, but he ignored it. "I'm done here. Can we move on to the lower-level public areas?"

John jumped up to open the heavy door at the end of the hallway. "Right through here."

"Is it always unlocked?" The man asked, pen poised.

"Always," John said. "It's a fire exit. They're all over the place. We have more unlocked doors than locked ones. Our insurance company insists on it."

Brady stroked his mustache, hiding a sympathetic grin. Encouraged, John led them through the door and into the lower-level lobby.

"This area is mostly just lounges. Men and women, you know. Men have the Egyptian lounge, and the women are Arabian. There are a few small meeting rooms, but as far as I know, they aren't used." John opened a door and looked inside. "Completely empty. Not even tables and chairs."

"This Arabian ladies' lounge…is it used by the staff?" Brady asked. "Should we get someone to go in and make sure it's empty?"

"Only guests are permitted to use it," John said. "There are others for the staff."

The police officer stopped at an alcove outside the arched doorway, frowning. "This dish full of marbles…are they valuable?"

"Of course, they're valuable," snapped the insurance man. "They're glass art by Vinderzi." He consulted his list. "One six-inch bowl and twenty-four assorted one-inch mineral orbs."

Michael poured them into his large hand and poked through them, ignoring the man's indignant squawk. "There are twenty-three here." He examined the recess and shook his head. "Someone took one of the balls, but that doesn't seem big enough to kill over."

"They're not balls or marbles. They're orbs." The insurance man circled the item on his list. "They would be easy to steal…no effort at all. A passerby could just slip one into her purse or his pocket and never even stop." He glared at John. "We would contest a claim for this loss, based on the location and lack of security."

John nodded. It was a bad place for them, but they looked good there. "I'll move them."

Brady poured the orbs back into the bowl. "Would one of them be valuable without the whole set?"

The man shrugged. "Not much. The thief was probably a theater guest who took it as a souvenir."

The Arabian ladies' lounge was similar in size and style to the rest of the lounges in the theater. They were all extravagantly spacious and luxurious, with writing desks and comfortable sofas. The one on the mezzanine level was notable for its elegant balcony. The insurance agent had been outraged to find the two enameled urns there full of cigarette ends. This one was clean, freshened by vases of spring flowers. Expensive vases, apparently, since the pen and clipboard were busy again.

"Excuse me, sirs. I didn't know you were in here." The cleaning woman—just a girl, really—dropped a stack of linens on a shelf and backed out of the lounge.

"Wait." John followed her. "You're Milly, right? Do you always take care of this area?"

"Yes, sir. All of the lounges."

The insurance man stepped forward. "Are you responsible for those flowers?"

Her eyes grew wide. "Yes, sir. They get delivered all arranged, and I put them in clean water. That's all."

"Never mind that." Brady touched her elbow, steering her

toward the bowl of orbs. "Did you know there's a marble missing?"

"Only one of them?" The girl's unexpected snort surprised John.

"There should be twenty-four," he said, "but there are only twenty-three."

"It's a wonder there are any at all," she said. "Ernie said she thought the ladies were picking them up for mementos."

Brady counted them again. "Twenty-three," he said. "It doesn't look like too many ladies were taking souvenirs."

"Ernie told Mr. Langdon because she didn't want him thinking it was one of us. She said he counted them and said they were all there. That was a while ago, though," she said, "before she died." She flushed. "I mean, it was a while before that."

"Were there other missing items?" The insurance man asked.

She hunched her shoulders. "She was always worried that we'd be blamed if things went missing. She told him off about the things being too easy to steal. She said it was an unfair temptation to human flesh."

John hoped he wasn't as red as she was. "Yes, but did she ever say anything to you or Mr. Langdon about specific items being stolen?"

She scratched her elbow. "Not just stolen. Everything is so breakable, and it's hard to clean it safely."

"Had something been broken?" The policeman looked at the girl from under lowered brows. "Something valuable?"

She was pale now, all color having left her face. "No, sir. Not that I know of. Ernie would have fired anyone who broke things, so we had to be careful."

John glanced up at Brady. "Maybe Ernie was killed by a clumsy housekeeper." He regretted the flippant comment as soon as he spoke it, even before the girl slid off the chair in a faint.

EIGHT

Clive Zech wasn't nearly as impressive offstage as he was during his vaudeville act. He fidgeted with the envelope he carried, and sweat glistened on his unpowdered face.

"You're the owner here, right?"

John nodded. "Yes, I am. Is there a problem?"

"I have something for Hewitt Langdon, but no one seems to know where he is. Do you have a forwarding address for him?"

"No," John said. "He's disappeared."

"I heard the police were looking for him, too," Zech said. "Is there a reason…I mean, are they looking for him because he disappeared, like a missing person, or for some other reason?"

"He's a missing person." John frowned. "Do you know anything about him?"

"No, no." Zech scratched his head with the corner of the envelope. "Never met him. He's supposed to have a package for me, for me to deliver to the agency."

"The insurance agency?" John asked, confused.

"No, no. The agency. Tobler and Jones."

"Maybe you should tell the police," John said. He hadn't heard anything from the detective in two days, so their investigations must have been fruitless. "That might be useful information."

Zech took a step backward. "Oh, it's probably nothing. Just an errand for the boss. Nothing to do with me at all."

"It might help them to know that he was expecting something and still took off," John said. The envelope was thick, more suggestive of a pile of cash than a document or letter. If Langdon had left voluntarily, wouldn't he have waited for the money?

"I'll just take this back to the boss. Probably a misunderstanding. Not my business."

Zech hustled away, and John headed toward his office. It had to be important in some way. He didn't know much about Langdon's life outside of the theater. The man had come with good references from three theaters, and he seemed to know the job.

He could be a gambler. That would explain the money, but what could he have been sending back to Tobler and Jones? The booking agency was in New York, wasn't it? He changed direction and headed toward the manager's office. It was time to deal with Miss Fisher, anyhow.

THE WOMAN WAS SPEAKING into the telephone, and her demeanor—rushed and frantic—indicated a personal rather than a business conversation.

"You need to find him. Now!" Her voice was angry and…frightened?

John cleared his throat, and she looked up. She turned visibly paler, eyes wide. She hung up the phone with a crash and then settled it more carefully into its cradle.

She gave a weak and unconvincing chuckle. "My cat. It ran away."

"Your cat and your boss," John said lightly. "You're having a bad time of things."

She thrust out her jaw. "The theater has run just fine since Mr. Langdon's been gone. I have it all under control."

"I know you do," he said. "I've seen that." He dropped into the chair opposite her desk and tipped his head toward Langdon's office door. "In fact, I'd say nothing has changed at all. Except Ernie's death, of course."

"Of course," she said. "Everything else is going smoothly. The reels for *My Lady of Whims* just arrived, and the publicists are working on the boards. I had to let two of the ushers go, because they were letting their friends in for free, and I've hired two more. Oh, and I replaced the carpet where Ernie… um, fell."

"I hadn't thought of that," John said, "but I suppose it was… It sounds like you have it all under control. What about a new head cleaning lady?"

She slapped her hand on the desk. "That was the most vexatious thing. I offered the job to one of the other cleaning women—a good promotion!—and she went into hysterics. She ran out of the office, howling."

"That's odd." John crossed one leg over the other knee and leaned against the back of the chair. "You don't know why?"

"No idea. All the other girls were too young, or they weren't responsible enough, so I telephoned to an agency. They've sent a few applicants, but I haven't hired anyone yet." Miss Fisher ran a finger over the base of the telephone. "Ernie must have trained the girls better than I'd realized, because the housekeeping department is doing quite well, all things considered. Aside from the hysteria, of course."

She seemed to be taking charge of the personnel. John

wondered if she'd been doing it even before Langdon left. Maybe she'd been doing more of his work than anyone knew.

"You know Miss Fisher, even if Mr. Langdon showed up tomorrow, I'm afraid he's lost my trust."

She inhaled sharply and sat up. "Yes, indeed, sir."

"And because you've been doing such a good job since he left, I think it only right that I offer you the job. The position of theater manager."

"Ohhh…" She drew out the word. "Even if he comes back?"

John nodded. "Whether he comes back or not. If he does come back, he's fired."

"What if his disappearance wasn't his fault?"

That was an odd question. John scratched his jaw. "I don't know about that. You mean, he might be injured and have amnesia or something like that? It seems unlikely. I think the police have asked around the hospitals for him. The morgues, too."

"But it's possible," she insisted.

"We'll reassess the situation if that is the case and he comes back." Didn't she want the job? "But we can't go on without a theater manager indefinitely."

Except that they'd been doing just fine without one for the past two weeks, thanks to Miss Fisher. "If you're interested in the job, it's yours. If you'd rather not do it, I'll look for someone else."

"Oh, no! I mean, I do want it. Thank you, sir. I won't let you down." She stood up, trembling a little, and clutched the table for support. "I'm grateful for the chance."

He stood, too. "It seems to me that you've been doing the job already, for a while."

"Yes, sir, I'm familiar with every part and responsibility of the position." She flicked a glance toward the other door, and John grinned.

"You'd better start moving your things into your new office and maybe begin looking for an assistant, too."

"Oh, yes! Thank you!"

"It's a well-deserved promotion." He extended a hand to shake hers. "I know you'll do a fine job."

A satisfied smile—the first sign of confidence he'd seen since he arrived—lit her eyes.

"I'll do my best."

He left the office, wondering what people would say about him hiring a woman for such an important job. She'd be good at it if people treated her with the respect she deserved. He'd have to watch that.

What would Gayle Wells think? She was one of the first female organists in the country, and now the Empire had the first female theater manager, too. His grandmother would be pleased.

John thought about the odd conversation he'd interrupted. A missing cat didn't seem to warrant such fear. She'd been angry, too, not just distressed. If she was particularly attached to her cat, she might be worried, but there had been something different than that in her tone.

The only missing person he knew of was Langdon, though, and why would Miss Fisher be talking on the telephone about him in that way? Maybe he shouldn't have been so quick to offer her the job.

NINE

"Oh, my." Gayle blinked at the boards, and the men installing them turned to grin at her.

"Clara Bow's the queen of shebas, for sure," the taller man said. He tipped his head and gazed admiringly at the scantily clad actress.

"She's a looker," the other man agreed, "but my own dame says I'd better be keeping my peepers closed when I'm putting up these pictures."

Gayle sympathized with his wife. *My Lady of Whims* had caused a stir in the newspapers, but she hadn't seen the pictures until now. She'd have to keep her own peepers closed while she played the organ.

"We'll be having that morality policewoman out here for sure," a familiar voice said, "and probably my grandmother."

She turned to smile at John Starek. "Marie Owens? I wouldn't be a bit surprised. She's a friend of my mother's. What happens if she decides your billboards are too risqué?"

"We'll paper over them in strategic areas with notices about the other shows," he said, "and be a little more careful about which movies we order in the future. We won't let kids into the show, or your Mrs. Owens will be out here policing the lobby."

Gayle pulled her scarf a little closer. "You could paint some clothes on her. She'll catch pneumonia in that…er, dress, in this weather."

He laughed. "We might have to do that. How do you feel about playing for it?" He gestured toward the billboard. "Would you prefer to take next week off work?"

She shook her head. "I can do it," she said. "I'm only doing matinees next week. Jesse and Mr. Shores are doing the evening shows."

"Marty Shores is doing a fine job," he said. "I'm glad we could give him work after he lost his job at the Roxy. We took on a few of their people." He smiled at her. "You do a good job, too, and we're glad to have you."

"Thank you, sir." She hadn't brought her complaints to him, and she hoped Miss Fisher hadn't. He didn't sound as if was trying to reassure her. It sounded like a simple observation, and it would be best to accept it as a compliment. "This new vaudeville troupe is entertaining," she said. "The acrobats are amazing."

"The Amazing Zandizi isn't amazing. He's a flop."

"The illusionist?" Gayle asked. "I thought he was good."

He huffed. "The agency told me he'd studied under Houdini, but I don't believe it. This man's an amateur. His illusions looked like tricks, his escapes were obvious, and his cabinet looked like it was falling apart. I don't think the agency ever saw his act, or they wouldn't have sent him here."

"His rabbit trick was good," Gayle offered. "I didn't expect the second rabbit."

"That was the only good trick he did, but he didn't get that from Harry Houdini. It's just a stunt." He touched her shoulder to direct her out of the way of the workmen. "Let's walk down this way."

Gayle complied. "You sound like quite a connoisseur of

illusionists. I'm glad you don't call him a magician, by the way."

"There's no such thing as magic," he said, "and Busia—my grandmother—scolded me when I used the word. Harry Houdini is opposed to it, too. He makes quite a big deal out of revealing tricksters who claim to talk to the dead. Spiritualists and mediums. Lately, he does more of that than his regular performances." He sounded disgruntled.

"My father read us an article in the newspaper a few months ago," Gayle said. "He said Mr. Houdini was doing good." She wrinkled her nose. "Lillian and I got in trouble one time, when she brought over her new Ouija board. She'd received it as a birthday gift and didn't know how to use it. My father was upset. Our argument that everyone else was doing it only made everything worse."

He smiled. "I can imagine. Your father is strict?"

"He's a minister," Gayle said, "and he feels even more strongly than Mr. Houdini does about the evils of spiritualism. It's awfully popular these days."

"Lillian is the woman who was with you in Miss Fisher's office the other day, right? And the police officer?"

"Lillian's my best friend. We've known each other all our lives. And in case you couldn't tell, the police officer is my brother-in-law. He was a little older than us, growing up, and we were terrible pests when he was dating my sister. He still thinks of us as pesky little girls."

"He did seem annoyed with the two of you," John said with a grin.

Gayle dug her gloves from her pockets and pulled them on. Michael was even more annoyed with her—quite unjustly—now that the police had found a lot of artwork missing from the theater. He'd told her to keep the marble until their investigation was finished and return it 'when the heat was off.'

"The police aren't telling us much." He grabbed at his hat as the wind caught it. "They've interviewed everyone in the theater, even poor Milly, the cleaning woman. She got hysterical, and Miss Fisher slapped her."

Gayle winced. "Did it help?"

"No, not at all. I've never understood how it might," he said. "The policeman decided she probably didn't know anything worthwhile, but it seemed to me that she was one of the few who might know something helpful. She's been at the Empire longer than the others, and she wouldn't be hysterical unless she knew something she didn't want to share, right?" He started walking again. "I don't want to criticize the woman, now that she's dead, but it sounds like Ernie was hard on the girls and had a sharp tongue. She just didn't get on with anyone here, so no one knows anything about her."

"Did she have family?" Gayle asked.

"Miss Fisher talked to her landlord, who said she didn't know of any friends or relatives. No one ever visited."

"How sad," Gayle said. "I can't imagine not having any family or friends."

"It's hard to imagine," John said, "but they haven't tracked down any relatives for Henry Glassman, either. He hadn't been at the theater all that long, and Miss Fisher says he moved here from New York."

"No friends or family for either of them," Gayle said.

"We took care of their final expenses, of course, but there wasn't anything else to do." He shoved his hands in his pockets. "I hope the police find the killer soon. The cleaning girls are all agitated, being convinced that there's a madman loose in the theater or that the Empire is haunted. One of them said she heard music and maniacal laughter coming from the basement late at night. Another claims to see shadows in the corridors, and then one said she saw Ernie's ghost. None of them will work late now, so they're coming in extra early in the morning instead."

"That's nice of you to let them."

"Not me." He held up both hands. "That's up to Miss

Fisher. As long as the place is ready in time for the matinee or whatever else is going on, I don't care when they do it."

The cool Miss Fisher wasn't likely to have patience with the superstitious fears of the housekeeping staff, Gayle thought. She'd be more likely to fire them, especially if she'd really slapped poor Milly for being in hysterics. It had most likely been John Starek's influence that caused her to accommodate the girls.

He cleared his throat. "I wanted to tell you…I promoted Miss Fisher to the theater manager position."

"Oh!" She stopped, turning to face him. "So, you're sure Mr. Langdon isn't coming back?" Gayle tried to be pleased for the woman. She might be unpleasant, but she deserved the promotion.

"It doesn't matter if he does come back," he said. "She's the new manager. I think she'll do a good job."

"She's probably been doing the job all along," Gayle said. "Assistants often do. At any rate, they know everything that's going on and get stuck with all the work."

"My secretary keeps me in line," John admitted. "I just do whatever she tells me. I'd be in trouble without Mrs. Barrow."

They turned the corner and continued on Clover Street.

"So, are you making friends here at the theater?" He asked.

"Not yet." Gayle glanced at the theater door, hoping no one would come out and see them walking together. "But I'm not alone like Ernie and Mr. Glassman. By the way, does Ernie have a last name?"

"That is her last name—Ernst. Her given name was Charity. She preferred to be called Ernie."

"I can't blame her," Gayle said.

"So, you haven't been making friends here?" he persisted.

"There aren't many women in the music department, are there? A few in the orchestra. Still, there are other female employees, and Miss Fisher."

Gayle smiled. "I assure you, I'm fine. I enjoy talking to others, but I stay busy outside the theater, too. Besides…"

When she didn't continue, he prompted, "Besides?"

She flexed her hands and then clasped them, turning to look directly at him. "It's hard to be the only woman—one of the only women—in the music department. Whenever I try to stand up for myself, they act like I'm a hysterical woman. They just aren't used to having women in the department."

He frowned. "That's not acceptable. You should be able to stand up for yourself. Have you talked to Jesse Erwin, as your union representative, or Bennet about it?"

"I'm afraid I had quite a row with Jesse Erwin the other day, and I don't think Mr. Bennet likes me either," she said. "The organ and the orchestra have always been all men, and it's just recently that women are taking those positions. Eventually, they'll adapt."

"You shouldn't have to wait for eventually," he said. "Maybe Miss Fisher should talk to them. Or maybe not. I could do it."

"Please don't. I think Miss Fisher talked to them. I'm not sure it helped, but that's okay." It wasn't really okay, but Gayle wanted to stop talking about it. "Do you get to request certain acts, like illusionists?"

He regarded her, brows knit, for a few seconds before replying. "I can request them, but the acts all have agents, and they usually work on circuits, traveling from one theater to another."

"So, you contact a booking agency?" She asked.

"The theater manager does. We usually work with United Booking or Tobler and Jones, in New York. We could do better, probably, but the syndicates get the top-notch acts first." He grinned. "All we have is Chicago's first lady organist."

TEN

It was a travesty. Why bother getting married at all? They'd be divorced in a year. The bride had wanted to be married in the new Union Station or a dance hall. Somewhere more interesting than a boring old church, she'd said.

Gayle tried to maintain the cheerful attitude of the frivolous lyrics. She tapped her foot to keep up the rhythm, forcing her gloomy thoughts to the back of her mind. How on earth had Lillian persuaded the minister to let her use this song? Maybe she hadn't. Asking forgiveness was easier than asking permission, and Lillian probably didn't care about forgiveness, anyhow. She wasn't a member of this congregation. Getting married in a church was her mother-in-law's idea.

An awkward smattering of applause broke the silence that followed her final notes. They hadn't done that after the hymn she sang before the prayers. Gayle nodded and stepped off the stage, returning to Lillian's side. No, not a stage. It was a platform in church. She was grateful it wasn't her own church, because the tight-lipped man in white robes was glaring at her as if her rendition of "You Are My Favorite Thing" was a mortal sin.

The pastor smoothed the fronts of his stole and returned his scowl to the bridal pair. Lillian smirked. Willie shifted from one foot to the other, obviously uncomfortable in the hallowed setting. Gayle stood, avoiding the eyes of the audience, trying to focus on the familiar wedding service. What would her father say? She should have warned him ahead of time. She'd meant to, but the perfect moment never arrived.

"Lillian and William, I invite you, at this time, to join hands and make your vows in the presence of God and His people." The man's voice was high-pitched and irritated. Gayle didn't blame him. She was a little irritated herself.

She would have wanted to be a part of Lillian's wedding, even with the ridiculous music, but she couldn't help feeling taken advantage of. Lillian had gotten her an audition at the Empire, but Gayle had earned the job on her own merits. Hadn't she? Lillian seemed to think it was something more. Gayle didn't like being beholden to her, especially when she was reminded every few days. If she hadn't owed her new job to Lillian, she could have put her foot down and refused to do the silly songs—maybe even persuaded Lillian to reconsider this hasty marriage.

SHE KNEW many respectable people drank alcohol. According to Lillian, people drank more during prohibition than they had before then. It didn't even have to be good alcohol, Lillian said. The cheap booze was part of the thrill. Dancing and gambling and cheap whiskey.

But somehow, Gayle hadn't anticipated that the upright and respectable Mrs. Fanshaw would serve it at the formal and elaborate wedding reception she'd insisted on. It was all champagne, of course, served in paper-thin flutes by an army of tuxedo-clad footmen and pouring from a fountain in a punch bowl on a table near the cake. It didn't look sanitary to Gayle.

Almost all the guests were drinking champagne, lifting their glasses in toast to the bridal couple. Others, including her own family, were sipping lemonade or soda water, cheering with the crowd, smiling, chatting and nodding.

Gayle watched her brother-in-law make his way across the room toward her and wondered how he felt about the party. Like many of the other Irish policemen, he didn't approve of prohibition, claiming it made criminals out of law-abiding citizens and was responsible for most of the violence in Chicago. He enjoyed discussing the issue, especially with his mother-in-law, but as far as Gayle knew, he didn't drink.

"How are you enjoying yourself tonight? That was a fine performance you gave at the church."

The teasing big brother was in evidence this evening—a welcome contrast to the suspicious policeman attitude.

"Those were all Lillian's songs—not mine," she said.

"You didn't have to sing them," he said, "but I know you have a soft spot for her." He turned to look at the dance floor, where Lillian and Willie were performing a waltz. "I hope she's happy." His words were sincere. "She runs with a bad crowd. Maybe marriage will settle her."

"Maybe," Gayle echoed. "I hope he's good to her. She deserves happiness."

"You should watch yourself, too," Michael said. "That theater crowd isn't much better. There's something going on there. Ashe is convinced that Langdon killed the cleaning lady, but I'm not so sure."

"It seems like the obvious solution," Gayle said. "Lillian keeps hinting that he had some dark secret, and she's still convinced he pushed her in front of that streetcar."

"Maybe so." Michael leaned closer, to be heard over the orchestra. "This is my chance for promotion, or to be noticed for promotion next year. If I could find Langdon or prove that someone else committed the murder…it would be a fine thing for me."

"You don't think Langdon left town already?" Gayle asked.

Michael shook his head. "He disappeared, but he stayed long enough to push Lillian—if he did."

"She's awfully certain."

"That's why I'm not so sure it's really Langdon," Michael retorted. "There's reasons."

Gayle tipped her head and regarded him. Michael really was a good policeman, and she was a civilian. "What kind of reasons? You can tell me. I promise I won't tell anyone else. Maybe I can give you some…insight, based on the people I meet at the theater."

She could see the indecision on his face. He'd never been able to keep a secret, even as a boy. She gave her most winning smile. "Come on, Mickey. You know you can trust me."

He blew out a breath. "Well, we visited Langdon's apartment, and if he did run off, he did it without his luggage. He left a lot of money—too much money for a theater manager—in the safe at the hotel, and a closetful of expensive clothes. The room was neat, and the maid said he hadn't slept in the bed since she made it last. She said he wouldn't have made it himself."

"That does sound strange," Gayle said. "Did he live alone?"

"All alone, and it was a pretty plush apartment for a single man. More expensive than a man in his position should have."

"I don't know anything about that," Gayle said, "but I would think he's well-paid."

"Not paid well enough for an apartment in that hotel or the money we found in his room and in the safe. Thousands of dollars, in fifty-dollar bills. There aren't a lot of legal ways to get that kind of money."

Michael wore his disapproving policeman look now, and Gayle decided to back off. He meant bootlegging or gambling, probably, not theft.

"Lillian said he might be hiding from someone," she offered. "You should talk to her."

Michael grunted. "Talking to Lillian is like chasing a butterfly. I think half the things she says are just to get attention."

"You know that's not true, Michael! She's just…"

"Wild," he finished. "She's sweet as pie with us, but she's not the same person in public."

Gayle couldn't deny it. She'd defended Lillian a thousand times over the years.

"Are you having a glorious time, old friend?" The bride swept in, her silver dress trembling with glass beads. Diamonds—or something similar — fringed her face. She looked happy, and Gayle's heart melted.

"It's a wonderful party, Lily."

"Thank you." Lillian looked around. "Mrs. Fanshaw had some good ideas." She flashed Michael a grin. "I hope you aren't going to arrest all of us. That would be an exciting end to our wedding day, though, wouldn't it?"

"I leave that up to the Prohis," Michael said, "with their disguises and tricks. Regular coppers have enough to do already."

Lillian shook her head. "Not at my party. No murdered cleaning ladies and disappearing theater managers here." She tapped his chest. "Go dance with Ruth. She looks lovely tonight."

"That she does." Michael nodded to both of them and strolled away.

The girls watched him go.

"He's not as doltish as he looks," Lillian said. "I think it's just that he's so big. That's deceiving." She turned back and grasped Gayle's hand. "I'm married! I'm married to Willie!"

Gayle couldn't remember the last time she'd seen Lillian so giddy. Never, as an adult. "I'm so happy for you, Lily. I know your parents are watching and rejoicing for you, too."

Lillian swallowed, dimming slightly, and Gayle regretted her impulsive words. "I'm sorry. I think they're glad you're happy, though. They'd want this for you." Gayle grinned. "Well, I'm not sure about all the champagne, or the wedding songs, but they would want you to be married and happy. And having babies!"

"Not yet! I've only been married a few hours!" Lillian gazed across the room, drawn as if by instinct to where her new husband stood. He looked up and smiled at her, and Lillian sighed blissfully. "I'm so lucky." She raised a perfectly penciled brow at Gayle. "You would say blessed instead of lucky, of course."

"I'd rather have God than Lady Luck managing my future," Gayle said. "Luck is notoriously fickle, and God is always the same. You know that, Lillian." She held up a hand. "But I won't lecture you tonight."

"Thank you." Lillian embraced her and stepped back. "You're the best friend ever."

"But not your favorite thing?" Gayle asked. She spotted Jesse Erwin approaching them, weaving slightly, as if he'd had plenty of champagne already. "You invited Jesse Erwin to your wedding?"

"Not me," Lillian said. "I can't stand him. I only invited your family. Everyone else was on Mrs. Fanshaw's list." She brushed the sparkling fringe away from her eyes. "But they all brought nice gifts. I don't remember Jesse's name on the list, so he probably came with one of the invited guests."

The organist took Lillian's hand and bowed over it. "I have offered my congratulations to your husband on securing such a lovely bride, and I must offer you my best wishes as well."

Lillian pulled her hand back more quickly than graciously. "Thank you. I believe you know my good friend, Miss Gayle Wells."

"Yes, indeed. I was not aware of the relationship, however." He nodded at Gayle. "You are fortunate to have such influential friends."

"Blessed," Lillian interposed. "You and I are lucky. Gayle is blessed." She plucked a champagne glass from the tray of a passing waiter and raised it in salute. "And I'm the grateful one. She was my bridesmaid and the musician, too."

"You did a fine job with the songs," Jesse said to Gayle. "You are obviously skilled at church music."

"I don't think you can call that church music." Gayle suppressed a desire to strike back with sarcasm. "I've never played 'You Are My Favorite Thing' or 'Sweet Little Kitten' in my own church."

"Ah, yes. Your father is a minister. That explains it. And, of course, you have some influential friends."

The barbs shouldn't have stung. She knew she was doing just fine at the Empire. Gayle lost the battle with her sinful nature and opened her mouth to let him have it.

"Oh, stop it, Jesse." Lillian swatted at his arm. "You're just jealous. Gayle's a great musician. She can play anything, from hymns to jazz music—on the organ!"

Not helpful. Gayle bit her tongue as Jesse's face darkened.

"I'm not as experienced as Jesse, though," Gayle said, instantly regretting the comment. Why was she placating him? Because it would keep the peace. She'd never been good at confrontation, and Lillian was right. Jesse was jealous. He was afraid she'd be more popular than he was.

"It requires more than experience," he said, "and a theater like the Empire doesn't usually hire novices. It was convenient for you that there was an unexpected opening, too. The competition is usually stiff."

Gayle lifted both shoulders in a shrug. "Mr. Langdon and Mr. Bennet thought I deserved the job."

But Mr. Bennet had already hired another organist. It was convenient to have free time for the wedding, but Gayle needed to work if she was ever going to be able to get her car. To that end, and to keep the peace at Lillian's wedding reception, she needed to be on good terms with Jesse.

He took a gold case from his jacket pocket and extracted a slim cigarette. "Langdon's gone now, and Bennet…well, Langdon usually doesn't do the hiring for the musicians. It was…unusual. Unprecedented."

Lillian shook her head. "You can't smoke in here. There's a balcony over there. Way over there, on the other side of the room." She pointed.

He put the cigarette back in the case and slid it back into his coat pocket. "Later. I've been wanting to ask you about that, Miss Nagle—Mrs. Fanshaw. About Langdon. I heard you say he pushed you in front of a streetcar, a week after he disappeared. I'm intrigued by the whole thing…the murder—more than one, if he killed poor Henry—and then his disappearance. His unusual involvement in hiring your friend, and then your accusations. It all seems very mysterious."

Connecting her with the murder? Gayle didn't have time to sort through the outrageous remarks before he went on. "And why should he kill the cleaning woman? Why disappear?"

A waiter appeared, and Jesse took a glass. He poured half of it down his throat and set the glass on a nearby table. "What kinds of secrets could he have had?"

Lillian fingered her pearls. "Everyone has secrets." She tapped Gayle on the arm. "Not you, darling, but everyone else."

Gayle rolled her eyes. Jesse snorted.

"The thing is," Lillian said, "it's so easy to move from one place to another and start a new life if you have enough money. You can pick a new name, if you want to, make up some references if you need a job, and start life all over again. All those theater people—the vaudeville people—do they use their real names? Do you know what they were doing five years ago?"

"Are you saying Langdon wasn't who he said he was?" Frowning, Jesse picked up his glass and drank the remainder of the champagne.

Lillian tipped her head and examined the pearls. "I have no idea. I didn't know him well in New York. You might ask Bennet if you're so curious."

"Gayle!" Dot arrived, sweeping the scene with a quick glance. "Congratulations, Lillian. It was a lovely wedding." She eyed Jesse's empty glass. "Except for the alcohol, of course. It's illegal, you know."

Lillian chuckled. "Thanks for letting me know, Dot. I will remember that next time." She shook her head. "No, there won't be a next time. One wedding, till death do us part."

"Mother and Papa are ready to go, Gayle," Dot said, "and they sent me to see if you need a ride home."

"It's still so early," Lillian objected. "You can't leave yet."

"It's after ten," Dot said. "They're outside, looking for you and Willie, to say goodbye."

"I'll come right now."

Jesse grabbed Lillian's wrist as she started forward. She gasped, and the three women stared at him. He released her immediately. "I apologize. I was just so interested in what you were saying. Can we discuss it further when you've said goodbye to your friends?"

Lillian shook her head. "This is my wedding day. I must find my husband and attend to our guests."

"But I want to know more," Jesse said. "Can I call on you tomorrow?"

"I'll be on my honeymoon!" Lillian turned her back on him and walked toward the door. "It was just gossip," she said over her shoulder. "Just idle gossip. Forget it."

Gayle watched Jesse's face and knew he wasn't going to forget it.

ELEVEN

"Are you the organist?" The Amazing Zambezi—Andrew Jenkins—stood in the doorway of the organ room and called to her, as if afraid to enter the room.

Gayle stood and gestured to the organ. "Yes, I am."

"Jones didn't say anything about you being a woman. I think he should have mentioned that."

"I'm not the only organist," she said, regretting her earlier sarcasm. "Are you looking for Jesse Erwin?"

"No, he said it wasn't Erwin. He said you worked with Langdon."

"Well, very briefly," Gayle said, "and I didn't exactly work with him. He hired me, and then he disappeared."

"Yeah, the disappearing is what's caused all the fuss." Jenkins pulled an envelope from his pocket stepped forward and thrust it into her hand.

She took it instinctively. It was sealed with old-fashioned sealing wax, with an imprint of theatrical masks. "For me?"

"Guess so." Jenkins turned to leave and ran into John Starek. "'Scuse me."

"Wait!" Gayle stepped forward and held out the envelope. "I don't think this is intended for me."

"Boss said to give it to you," the man said. "I'm just the delivery boy."

"No!" She shoved it toward him.

Jenkins heaved an exaggerated sigh and accepted the envelope. "Okay, okay, but the boss won't be happy. If I were you, I'd telephone him right quick and make some explanations."

"I have no idea what you're talking about!" she said.

The man glanced between her and John Starek. "Oh, right. He must have meant someone else. Sorry about that. Mistaken identity."

She scowled at his implication. Jenkins nodded to John and hastened away. A faint aroma of hair tonic lingered.

"What was that about?"

"I have no idea." Gayle sat on the organ bench. "None at all. He came in and started shoving that envelope at me. He said he was looking for the organist. Not Jesse."

"What about Shores?"

Gayle flushed. "I'd forgotten about him at first, but then Mr. Jenkins said I'd worked with Mr. Langdon. Not that I did," she added hastily, "but Mr. Shores wasn't here at all before Mr. Langdon disappeared."

"True. I wonder why he thought you did."

Her heart was beating too fast. She didn't have anything to hide, but Jenkins had surely made him suspicious.

"I don't know. I can't imagine." She spun to face the organ and shuffled the sheet music. "It was ridiculous. I need to get ready for the show. The button here is stuck, so Mr. Wilkes is operating the lift from the projection room. He'll do it at exactly eleven, whether I'm ready or not." She glanced at him over her shoulder. "Did you need me for something?"

"Oh, no. I just wanted to tell you that we put some additional clothing—announcements of upcoming attractions—on Miss Bow." He waved. "See you later!"

Gayle watched him go, pondering the situation. Did he really come down to tell her that? She wished he hadn't seen the odd exchange with Andrew Jenkins. She felt unreasonably guilty about it. Mr. Jenkins's departing words had made it all worse.

She sat up straight, flexed her hands, took few deep breaths, and thought about Mary Pickford. The trick wasn't working today; she couldn't shake the uneasy feeling something was wrong.

TWELVE

Gayle cleared her throat, not wanting to startle the middle-aged woman at the desk. Mrs. Barrow looked up and smiled warmly, beckoning her in.

"Miss Wells! Come in. Mr. Starek is talking on the telephone right now, but he'll be available in a few minutes." She pointed at a tapestry-covered chair.

"Thank you." Gayle perched on the chair and looked around. The secretary's office was considerably less ornate than her boss's. Her table was carved wood, not marble, and there were vases instead of statues. A mosaic globe, at least three feet across, was mounted in one corner.

"That is beautiful," she said. "I've never seen one so big."

"Isn't it?" The secretary rose and came around her desk to touch it. "Sometimes, I like to give it a spin, just for the pleasure of watching the lights."

Gayle laughed. "How could you resist? I would do that, too."

"Go ahead." The woman stepped back and gestured.

"Really?" Gayle grinned and rose. She laid a hand on the side of the globe and spun it. The light from the window and chandelier caught on the bits of inlaid marble and glass, sparkling and gleaming as the globe turned. "It's beautiful," she repeated. "A treasure."

"Mr. Starek's windows are stained glass, so he thought it would look better in here."

"That makes sense," Gayle said. "This theater is full of beautiful things, everywhere."

The secretary chuckled. "Have you seen those hanging baskets and urns of flowers outside?"

"I think so," Gayle said. "Yes."

"Mr. Starek didn't think anyone was noticing them, in their hurry to get inside, so he hung little chimes among them to get people's attention."

"The gardener worked hard on them, and no one ever stopped to see them." John Starek walked across the room, his steps muffled by the thick carpet. "They have to be put away in winter, too, so there's a limited time to enjoy them."

"Don't say that," Gayle said. "Summer has finally arrived! Winter was too long this year."

"Yes, that's what I want to talk to you about. Come into my office, so I can explain."

Explain why winter had lasted so long, as if it was his fault? Gayle followed him, smiling at the thought. Not even the Emperor had that power. She settled into a chair, watching him as he walked back to the secretary's room to request coffee. She'd never known anyone very wealthy, but John must be an exception to the usual. He liked to gather beautiful, expensive things, but then he wanted to show them off—not as a sign of his personal worth, to make others envious, but just to share them with anyone who would appreciate them. He derived pleasure from watching happy people.

His massive desk chair fit just right when he sat, filling it with his personality as much as his body. John pulled a suede-covered book from a drawer and flipped it open on the desk.

"I'm afraid this will sound like dreadful cheek, but I have a favor to ask of you. You will get paid, of course," he added quickly, "and you don't have to say yes if you don't want to." He ran a finger over the loosely written words on the page.

It must be his own writing—sprawling but legible. Even upside down, Gayle could read it. She lifted her gaze, but he was reading, too, as if he'd never seen it before.

"Yes? I mean, what is it?" Gayle asked.

"My grandparents are celebrating their fiftieth wedding anniversary next week, and suddenly, my grandmother has decided she wants to get married in a church. They are married, of course. They got married in Warsaw before they came to America. Perfectly legal and morally correct." One corner of his mouth quirked in a grin. "My grandfather keeps telling her that—legal and morally correct. He says they're already married in God's eyes, but Busia wants a wedding, and isn't he willing to marry her?"

"I think that sounds fun," Gayle said. "And romantic."

"I don't think Dziadzia—my grandfather—sees it as romantic, but he'll do anything to please her, so he's hired someone to help her plan a big party in Lake Geneva, with a wedding in a church. I'm pretty sure there won't be a string of flower girls and bridesmaids, and I hope she won't wear a fancy white dress, but you never know, with my grandparents. Just when I think they're old-fashioned and stuffy, they spring something like this on me. A few years ago, they went up in a hot air balloon, and then Busia learned to drive and my grandfather bought her a Duesenberg coupe. He wanted to buy an airplane, too, but Grandma put her foot down on that one."

"Your grandmother drives a coupe?" Gayle leaned forward.

John nodded. "Her driving is a bit alarming. The car has a loud horn that she uses freely for every purpose, from hailing a friend to indicating displeasure with another driver. Or announcing her intention to turn or informing the traffic policeman that she's not going to follow his direction."

Gayle laughed. "Does she get fines and lectures from the traffic police?"

"Are you jesting? My grandmother is a lovely Christian woman, but she still fails occasionally in the area of humility and patience. I'm afraid any lecturing is done by her—not the police," John said. "But she always feels guilty afterward."

"My father says that guilty feelings are a step in the right direction," Gayle said. Her father usually followed that up with comments on the difference between feeling sorry and repentance, even seeking forgiveness, but that homily didn't seem appropriate for the conversation. "So, they're having a wedding?"

"Yes, and even though it's short notice, they'll get a lot of people there. They're getting married in the Presbyterian church, and they've rented one of the big hotel reception halls for the dinner and party afterward."

She nodded, waiting.

"The thing is…" John ran a finger around the inside of his collar. "My grandma is a bit of a feminist when it suits her. She heard about you—the lady organist at the Empire—and came to one of your shows. I didn't even know she'd done that until she told me last night that she wants you to play for the wedding. Play the organ, I mean, and she asked if you could sing."

"Play for your grandparents' wedding?" Gayle blinked. "In Lake Geneva?"

"Yes. You can stay at their home—there's enough room for a dozen guests—or you can stay at the Villa Geneva. She said you weren't to stay anywhere cheaper." He laughed. "I think she liked you, even just from watching one performance. Oh, she said she'd met your mother a few times, at various events and meetings. Social work, I suppose. At any rate, she approved of you. That's a great honor." His grin kept the statement from sounding condescending.

"I don't know," Gayle said. "How long would I have to be

gone?" Mr. Shores would jump on the chance to take over more of her shows.

"We'd leave Friday morning. The wedding is on Saturday, and we'd come back on Sunday."

"We?"

"You could ride with me, in my motorcar," he said, "or you could take the train, but it's a pleasant drive by car."

Gayle considered that. John was an interesting man, but traveling such a distance with him and then staying in his grandparents' home would definitely cause gossip at the theater. She didn't need any more attention. She didn't know how her father would respond to the idea, either.

"It might be easier if I take the train," she said.

"How could it be easier? It would be more comfortable and more convenient by car."

There was no doubt of that. "Can I let you know tomorrow? I have to look at my schedule."

"Oh, we'll clear your schedule. At least, your work schedule. I don't know if you have other commitments." John leaned back into the chair. "My grandmother told me to pay you one hundred dollars for the weekend. You'd be expected to play for the wedding, but not for the reception. If you don't want to stay with us, your travel expenses and hotel bill will be paid by them, as well as a stipend for meals."

"Oh." A hundred dollars would bring her savings account to the goal, and she'd be able to buy that Gray touring car. Maybe even a different car if she looked around for a good price. "That's very generous. I'll let you know tomorrow morning. I need to talk to my parents." She wished she could clarify that she was seeking advice, not permission, but he seemed to accept the statement.

"That would be fine. I hope you'll come. My grandmother is set on having you, and she wants you to have a good time there, too."

Gayle dropped her portfolio bag inside the door and sighed at the sound of Lillian's laughter. Her friend could be counted on for opinions, but her advice would be slanted toward having a good time.

"I'm home!" She entered the kitchen to find Lillian sitting on a stool in front of the Hoosier, snapping peas into a bowl. Dot sat at the table, holding a newspaper as if it might bite her, reading something that didn't entertain her as much as it did Lillian.

They both looked up when she entered. Lillian held up a pea.

"See what a paragon of domesticity I am? Next thing you know, I'll be baking apple pies and washing dishes."

"You don't wash dishes?" Dot asked. "What does your husband think of that?"

"Well, I wash them sometimes," Lillian conceded, "but we have a woman who comes in twice a week, so I can leave them that long. Besides, we eat at restaurants."

"That's applesauce. You know how to cook," Gayle said. She sat and nodded at the newspaper. "What's happening?"

"The raiding of the nightclub behind the Martingale Hotel," Lillian said. "The patrons all escaped through a back door, and the alcohol—if there ever was any alcohol—was nowhere to be seen. The reporter seems to think the police were suspiciously clumsy and slow, perhaps giving everyone time to dispose of the evidence and get away."

Dot folded the newspaper and laid it aside. "The police are supposed to be enforcing the laws."

"Not prohibition," Lillian said. "That's up to the prohibition agents. The police say they have enough work to do. Even Mickey says that. I've heard him."

Dot scowled. "Prohibition is the law, so they ought to enforce it."

"They do, sometimes." Lillian bit into a pea. "They may not have arrested anyone, but the Silk Tuxedo is shut down."

"They'll just pop up again somewhere else," Dot said. "It's like a hydra, where you cut off one head and it grows two more."

"That's a good comparison!" Lillian ate another pea. "So, following that logic, the police—or the Prohis—should stop closing down the speakeasies."

"It's not just the drinking," Dot said. "That's bad enough, but there's gambling and…inappropriate shows."

Lillian hooted with laughter. "Inappropriate shows?"

Dot's red cheeks revealed her discomfort. "You know what I mean."

"I do." Lillian slid off the stool and gave Dot a hug. "And you're right about that. When I've been in places like that, I just walked out. It's hard to tell, ahead of time, what a club will be like. I think some of those girls are hoping to catch the eye of someone important and break into show business. The real show business, not the kind of show they're putting on now." She wrinkled her nose. "And some of them are just doing it because they're hungry."

"We have to stop that," Dot said. "That's what our social reform club at school is working on now—helping women so they don't have to earn money in places like that. Or worse."

Gayle decided it was time to intervene. Once Dot got started on her social reform movement, she wouldn't stop. She'd get back around to the drinking and nag Lillian. Lillian would get defensive and mock Dot's ideals. Dot would get mad, and they'd start bickering until one of them stormed out.

"I had an interesting invitation today. A job offer from John Starek to play the organ at his grandparents' wedding anniversary. They're having a church wedding after being married for fifty years."

"The Levines? Yes, you should do it!" Lillian said. "Willie's mother is going, and she asked us to go with her. I didn't want to, but if you're going, it will be fun. Willie says their place on the lake is great. They have their own boat. I think he wanted to go, but…" she shrugged. "I'm not real accustomed to that kind of society. You can stay with us at their house!"

That changed everything. It wouldn't be so awkward at the theater, if she were going with Lillian, and she wouldn't have to stay at a hotel alone or with John's grandparents—neither of which options appealed to Gayle or would please her parents.

"You don't think his mother would mind?"

"Oh, no. She'd probably be glad to know I have some respectable friends," Lillian said.

"She probably remembers me from the wedding," Gayle said, "and may not think of me as respectable."

Lillian waved her hand. "I took all the blame for that, and she knows your father is a minister."

Dot rolled her eyes. "That's what it takes to be respectable?"

"She will love you. How could she not?" Lillian spun in a circle, her pleated skirt flaring out around her knees. "It'll be the berries, with you there."

"But I'm so respectable," Gayle teased. "Won't I put a damper on your fun? Be a wet blanket?"

"No, you're the cat's pajamas. The bee's knees!" Lillian gave her a hug and resumed her perch on the stool, hooking the heels of her shoes on the crossbar. "I can't wait to tell Willie. I hope he's done soon."

Gayle crossed to the sink and turned the taps. "I hope he doesn't mind me tagging along. The streetcar was filthy today. It was crowded, so I had to stand, and the handrail was sticky."

"When you get your own car," Lillian said, "you won't have to worry about that."

"That's the best thing about this job offer. They're paying

me one hundred dollars! With what I already have saved, I can get the car right away!"

"That's very generous," Dot said, "but you won't want to drive yourself into the city every day. Where would you park?"

"I don't care if I have to park six blocks away," Gayle said, "if I can avoid the streetcar." She rolled the cake of soap in her hands. "I think I need a bath. Nothing but full immersion is going to work. My skirt got dirty, too. Think of all the savings in laundry once I'm driving my own clean car!"

"It's an extravagant purchase," Dot said. "Papa has a car already, and he can take you places that aren't on the streetcar lines."

"Now who's being a wet blanket?" Gayle said. "You know I've been saving for this for a long time."

"Think of all the good you could do with that money," Dot said.

"Think of all the Ford employees who depend on car sales," Lillian retorted. "That's good, too."

Dot snorted.

"Are you staying for supper?" Gayle asked.

"No." Lillian ate another pea. "Just waiting for Willie. He had an appointment with your father, so I came along, of course."

"Of course." Gayle took the bowl of peas. "Do try to leave some for our dinner—and I'm sure there's enough dinner for you to join us." She looked at the bowl. "We'll cook up some canned peas to go with these."

"Nasty." Lillian slid off the stool and shuddered dramatically. "I loathe canned peas."

"You don't have to eat them," Dot said, "if you don't want to. We're having a roast chicken, new potatoes with cream sauce, buns, and peas. Ice Box Cake for dessert. There's plenty."

"Maybe another time," Lillian said. "I'd like Willie to get

to know all of you. Except for Gayle and at the wedding, he's hardly talked to any of you."

"And Papa, apparently. He had an appointment?" Gayle asked. She couldn't imagine what it was about. Willie was the epitome of flaming youth, up for any mischief and not interested in any of the things her father cared about.

"I don't know, but it's an improvement over his regular companions." Lillian sniffed. "We went to a party the other night and lasted about ten minutes before it got out of control. We left and went for a walk on the pier."

Interesting. Gayle reached around her to open the cabinet. "What was wrong with the party?" She held up a hand. "No, don't tell me. If it was bad enough that you and Willie walked out, I don't want to know."

They all turned at the sound of male voices in the hallway. Both men looked pleased.

"Hello, baby." Willie bounded over to give Lillian a kiss. "Thanks for waiting for me."

"Not a problem."

Gayle was amused to see that her friend's cheeks were slightly pink. "Lillian is always welcome here. She's like family."

"That's what she said," Willie said. "Said you were her oldest friend. Er, the friend she'd had the longest."

"Lillian is a friend to all of us," her father said, "and she's always welcome in our home. Will you both stay for dinner?"

Willie shook his head. "Not tonight, thanks."

The men shook hands and parted at the door, Lillian catching Willie's hand as they walked to the car.

"That was odd," Dot said. "I wonder what that was about."

"Ask Papa," Gayle suggested.

"Ask me what?" Her father entered the kitchen and took a pea from the bowl. He ate it and reached for another. "If it's about William, you know I can't tell you, so don't ask."

Gayle took the bowl and poured the peas into a pan. "I won't. I have something else to tell you." She perched on the stool Lillian had vacated. "I have a job offer—an overnight gig—out in Lake Geneva."

Her father raised his brows. It was his patient, inquiring eyebrow expression, so she continued.

"John Starek, from the theater, asked me to play the organ for his grandparents' second wedding."

He listened as she explained, ending with the information that she could travel and stay with Lillian and Willie, emphasizing that Mrs. Fanshaw would be present. Her father might not be impressed with the young couple as chaperones—not that she needed one, but he'd probably rather have a real adult there.

"That's a lot of money," he said. "And you want to do it?"

"Yes, I think so. I haven't been to Lake Geneva since we went there for summer camp, and then it was really a camp, with cabins. It would be fun to go and stay in a nice house and go to the party. I don't imagine it will get too riotous, since it's for Mr. Starek's grandparents."

"I've heard of them. They were—are—Jewish and became Christians later. They contribute a lot of money to things your mother is interested in. The grandson is the owner of the theater, isn't he?" Her father rubbed the back of his neck. "There was a murder there. Maybe two?"

Gayle hunched her shoulders in a shrug. "The first one isn't likely." She'd rather believe Mr. Glassman's death was an accident since it had opened the job for her.

"I met the man once," her father said. "The newspapers reported it as an accident."

"I'm sure it was," Gayle said. "They're only looking into it because of the coincidence in that they were both employed by the Empire. I can't see why anyone would murder Ernie, either. She was just a cleaning woman."

Her father's raised eyebrows indicated displeasure this

time. "She was a person, regardless of her career and social status."

"And it sounds like her work conditions were unsafe," Dot said. "Someone should be held accountable for that. Probably your Mr. Starek."

"She was doing something she shouldn't have. Ernie was supposed to wait for the maintenance man to move things for her, but she didn't. She was leaning out over the railings to reach something she didn't need to dust." Gayle didn't know why she felt compelled to defend John Starek, since she had openly accused him of the same thing. "She even had a longer duster that she could have used, but she didn't want to take the time to go get it from the supply room."

Gayle supposed John Starek still had some degree of responsibility, but it didn't seem fair to accuse him of negligence. If anyone was at fault, it was Hewitt Langdon. He was the theater manager—or rather, he had been, at that time. He should have seen what Ernie was doing at some point.

"Well, it really doesn't matter now, except that I hope Mr. Starek will make sure her family is provided for," her father said.

"She didn't have a family," Gayle said, "but he paid for her funeral."

"Good, good. Is dinner almost ready? Where's your mother? I've had a…rewarding day, and I'm hungry."

THIRTEEN

Gayle lifted away the paper and shook out the blue dress, relieved when the beading fell into place without snagging on the fabric. Working at the theater was certainly improving her wardrobe. She would never have purchased such an impractical garment on her own, but it was the perfect dress for tomorrow's event.

The silvery beading caught the light and sparkled, as if winking, telling her the dress was worth every penny.

No doubt. Gayle hung it in the wardrobe and turned back to the bed. The matching shoes, each in its own little bag, could remain in the suitcase, but the other gown needed to be hung up, too, until it was time to change clothes to go to the church.

This one was simpler, a rose-colored dress of artificial silk, with sheer sleeves and a draped bodice. The ivory satin sash wrapped her hips and hung lower than the hem of the skirt. She had pearls to wear with it—not real ones, of course, but they were good enough—and a trio of pearl bracelets to wear over her ivory gloves.

Gayle held up the dress in front of herself and twirled. It was exciting to be dressing up for a party instead of for work.

"Miss Wells?" The middle-aged maid at the door smiled indulgently. "That is a lovely dress. Can I help you unpack or take your luggage away?"

"Oh, no, thank you." Gayle felt herself blush. "I can manage. I only have one suitcase. It can stay here until Sunday, can't it?"

"Certainly." She pointed at a panel near the door. "If you need anything at all, press the top button, and someone will come up to assist you."

"Thank you." She would die first. Did Lillian press a bell and wait for a maid to attend to her?

Gayle strolled to the church, relishing the beautiful weather, enjoying Lake Geneva. The sun shone here, a pleasant change from the perpetual rain they'd been having in Chicago. People smiled and nodded as they passed. It smelled clean, too, with a warm breeze carrying flowers and trees with an undercurrent of fresh lake water. Just a week ago, she'd been fighting freezing rain.

Her pleasant reverie was interrupted by John Starek, waving and calling her name. She sighed, wishing she could stay outdoors a little longer before entering the dim church. This was what she had come for, though, so she smiled brightly and waved back.

"You're here!" John held the door for her. "I want you to meet my grandparents before we start the rehearsal."

Gayle grinned at the word. John's grandmother wanted a church wedding—a belated blessing on their marriage—but she wanted to put on a show, too. A rehearsal was appropriate.

"I'm not late, am I?" She twisted her arm to check her watch, and her portfolio slid off her shoulder, its contents spilling onto the polished floor.

They both squatted on the floor, Gayle minding her skirt

and cautious about her modesty, to scoop up the mess. She picked up the small bag of makeup first, shoving it into the bag with an embarrassed chuckle. John scooped up papers, stacking and tapping them on the floor to straighten them. A slip of paper fell from the sheaf, and he handed it to her without comment, continuing to gather the sheet music and notes.

"Oh, that's not mine." Gayle handed the bill back to him. "It must have fallen from your pocket."

He pulled a thin wallet from his pocket and checked inside. "No, I wasn't carrying any loose money. It came out of your bag." He tried to give it to her, but she pulled back.

"Really, it's not mine. If I did have fifty dollars, I wouldn't carry it loose, either."

"It came from your bag," he said. "Maybe one of your parents put it in there, as a gift for your travels?"

"I don't think so." Her father had handed her a ten-dollar bill before she left the house, and she'd folded it carefully, tucking it into one of the shoe bags. Could her mother have slipped the fifty-dollar bill into her bag, as a surprise?

"Well, it's not mine," John said, "and it was mixed in with all your other papers, so you'll have to keep it."

"I don't think I should." Gayle accepted it, uncertain, but not wanting to continue arguing as they crouched on the floor in the foyer of the church. She could turn it in to the minister here later, if her mother didn't know anything about it.

John stood, hoisting the bag onto his own shoulder, offering a hand to help her rise. "I'll set your bag on the organ bench and then introduce you to my grandparents. My grandmother is having a wonderful time setting everything up. She's been looking for you."

"Am I late?" Gayle asked again. "I thought you said six o'clock, and it's still ten minutes to. Or did you want me here earlier?"

"Six o'clock," he said. "I was just looking forward to

seeing you. I was disappointed that you aren't staying at our house, but I'm sure the Fanshaws are making you comfortable."

"Oh, yes. It's a lovely house, and Mrs. Fanshaw is very kind." Kinder than Gayle had expected, and more careful of Lillian's feelings, hardly cringing at all at her friend's appearance and conversation.

"I should have asked if you needed a ride from their house," he said. "How did you get here?"

"Willie and Lillian are out on his boat. They dropped me at the pier, and they'll pick me up at eight."

"That's awfully early!" John looked disappointed. "I could drive you back in my car."

"They'll be waiting for me at eight," Gayle said, "and they're going to teach me how to play mahjong tonight. I think I'm the only person left on earth who's never played it."

"Good evening!"

John turned to greet his grandmother. "Busia, this is Gayle Wells. Miss Wells, my grandmother, Golda Levine."

A tall, striking woman with dark brows and snow-white hair, Mrs. Levine clasped Gayle's hand and smiled warmly. "My dear, I am so grateful you've agreed to play the organ for us. You play marvelously at the theater, and I was certain you were just the right person for us. Did John tell you I know your mother?" She tipped her head, hooded brown eyes fixed on Gayle's face. "Not well, but we've worked in some of the same organizations and projects. She is a strong woman. I was glad to get her daughter for my wedding."

Gayle's mother was certain they'd never met, and her father only knew the Levines by reputation. Gayle smiled and nodded.

"Thank you for inviting me. I've never played for such an interesting event, and it was kind of you to invite me to the reception afterward, too."

"Of course! I hope you enjoy it. I've had a wonderful time

planning it." Mrs. Levine turned and waved an arm, beckoning a man to join them. "Abraham, this is Miss Wells, who is playing the organ for us. Miss Wells, my husband Abraham Levine."

"It's a pleasure to meet you." They both spoke at the same time as they shook hands. Mr. Levine laughed heartily. "It's good of you to join us. We've heard much about you from our John."

Gayle cast a swift glance at John, who reddened slightly.

"You're our first female organist," he said, "almost the first one in the country. At least, the first trained one, in a major movie palace."

"I'm sure it's been difficult," his grandmother said, "working with all those men. Do they give you a hard time?"

"It's not too bad."

"Truly?" Golda Levine narrowed her eyes, watching her.

"Well, it is hard sometimes," Gayle admitted. "They aren't used to having a woman taking a job that's usually held by a man, and it's a competitive field, because the organist becomes something of a celebrity."

"Ah, are they jealous?" Mrs. Levine seemed to have forgotten the occasion, giving her full attention to Gayle without regard for the minister or other people waiting for her.

"It's hard," Gayle said, "because I'm a novelty. People come to see the 'lady organist.'"

"You're a good organist," John said, "not just a novelty."

"And you're young and beautiful," his grandmother went on, "and talented, but not arrogant or too showy."

She wasn't beautiful, but Gayle appreciated the second part of the compliment, glad she'd insisted on being Mary Pickford instead of Theda Bara. "I'm grateful for the opportunity."

"My dear girl." Mrs. Levine touched Gayle's arm. "You got the job at the Empire because of your skill. Have confidence in that. You are doing John a favor by drawing in new people."

John nodded. "Yes, I'm the one who's grateful."

No longer certain she had landed the job on her merits, Gayle just nodded. "Thank you. I'd better familiarize myself with the organ now. I brought the music you requested, and I'm ready to play, but all organs are a little different."

"This one won't have the toy box or all the tabs," John said. "No train whistles or horse's hoof beats. You might find it a bit dull."

She laughed. "I still play the organ at church most Sundays," she said, "without any train whistles."

Abraham Levine took his wife's arm. "Come, Golda. I want to get married before you change your mind and run off with a more interesting fellow."

Gayle watched them go. Plenty of marriages, like Willie and Lillian's, started with romance and excitement. The Levines' marriage, like her own parents', was the kind of relationship she hoped to have some day—one that grew richer over the years instead of just comfortable and dull.

"They're more like parents to me than grandparents," John said. "My mother died when I was born, and my father couldn't care for a newborn baby, so he let Busia take over. Even as I got older, they did most of the hard work. Eventually, my father remarried, and since his new wife was only ten years older than me, it was more comfortable with them."

"They seem like lovely people."

"Busia liked you," John said. "I knew she would. Here you go. Do you need anything? Better light?"

"No," Gayle said. She switched on the lamp and pulled the music from her portfolio. "Oh, dear." She'd forgotten it was all shuffled together. "Thank you for your help."

He accepted the dismissal and walked away to join his grandparents. Gayle organized the sheets of music, carefully separating them, afraid she might miss one or get them out of order. She didn't want to ruin the wedding by confusion in the music, especially after Mrs. Levine's kind words.

She did deserve her job, not because she was a woman, but because she was a good organist with good training. Lillian's influence had secured the audition, but what then? Mr. Bennet hadn't seemed overly impressed with her performance. Mr. Langdon had been the one to push for her employment.

Lillian had talked ominously about Langdon, hinting at a murky past. Her comments to Jesse at the wedding reception—obscure hints of changed names and secret lives—were worrisome, too. If she knew a secret about Mr. Langdon, Lillian was fully capable of bullying him into giving Gayle a job. No, not bully. Blackmail. Rubbing her temples, Gayle faced the word.

When Lillian had fallen into the street, she'd been certain Hewitt Langdon had pushed her. That would make sense if he thought she might reveal something he didn't want known.

What about Ernie? Could she have known something bad about Mr. Langdon, too? And Henry Glassman?

Where was Langdon now? Could he have panicked after failing to kill Lillian, afraid she would expose him? But Lillian hadn't. She'd just stalked around, making veiled accusations.

Gayle shook out the bound sheet music for "The Voice that Breathed O'er Eden" and sat, shocked, when two more bills fell from its pages. She glanced around quickly, to be sure no one was watching, and bent to pick them up. Fifty-dollar bills. This was not a gift from her mother. Lillian might have made her a gift of it, but she would have given her the money directly and insisted she accept it.

She checked carefully as she sorted the rest of the music, but there were no more. How had they gotten into her portfolio? She carried the bag wherever she went. It often sat on the floor, open, as she practiced, and she shoved it in her locker when she was performing. The money couldn't have been in there long; she would have noticed it.

She checked her watch. Were they waiting for her? No, the bride and bridegroom were still in conversation with the minister. Gayle picked up the money and added it to her makeup bag. She must remember to not open that except in the privacy of her room back at the Fanshaws' house. That maid might come in, too. She'd have to hide the money until she knew what to do with it. There couldn't be an innocent reason for it to be in her possession.

FOURTEEN

Gayle looked around the ballroom. "Well, the music is nice, but it's not as…decorative as the Empire."

John grinned. "You mean it's not as tacky. My grandmother says it's ostentatious and heathen."

"All that Egyptian decor?"

"Egyptian, Moorish, Greek…anything exotic." He gave a little shrug and admitted, "I like it. Besides, it makes people happy. For the price of a ticket, they can see things they've never experienced before—things that only rich people could afford before."

Gayle wondered if he'd had beautiful things in his younger years, or if his life had been more austere and practical. The rumors said he'd always been wealthy, born with a silver spoon in his mouth. He didn't act snobbish, and he seemed to find genuine, simple pleasure in making people happy. He was the nicest person she'd met at the theater so far.

"Did you design it yourself?"

"Oh, no." He shifted to face her. "Haven't you heard the history of it?"

"I haven't heard anything except that your grandfather gave it to you."

"Conditionally," John said. "I have to make a go of it. Dziadzia thinks that a man should do some kind of work for his money. I'm not dependent on it, though." He chuckled. "I couldn't afford the Gold Bug if I only had the theater to support me."

"I suppose not." Gayle sighed. "It's a wonderful car. I've been saving for a Gray touring car, but I wasn't making much progress until your grandparents' generous gift. Our neighbor is buying a new Buick, and I'm hoping to buy his Gray before he gets tired of waiting for me and sells it to someone else."

"Those are good cars. Solid. And it wasn't a gift. It was payment for your service."

She ignored that. "I don't see you driving one."

"I'm grateful for what I have, but if I couldn't afford an expensive car, I'd get a Gray. Maybe a Flivver."

It was hard to imagine John Starek without money. Gayle turned the topic back to the theater. "So, if you didn't build the Empire, did your grandfather?"

"Oh, no. My grandfather's a banker. The Empire was originally built as a community center and North American headquarters for the Imperial Grand Council of the Venerable Brotherhood of Peers of the Eastern Mystic Temple."

"The Imperial what?" Gayle asked, incredulous.

"The Imperial Grand Council of the Venerable Brotherhood of Peers of the Eastern Mystic Temple." He rolled the syllables off his tongue with obvious pleasure. "They raised money for it, and my grandfather says they would have been fine if they'd stuck to the original plan, but they kept adding more rooms and details, and they wanted all the most expensive materials. They wanted rich carpets and crystal chandeliers everywhere, even in the back rooms and small offices, and it went over budget. Way over budget. They raised some more money, but it wasn't enough, and they were still trying to expand it, so they came to my grandfather, who bailed them out with a loan. They couldn't make their payments, so the next time they asked him for money, he wanted a piece of the building."

"A piece of the building?"

"Part ownership," John explained, "and once he held a share in it, he started bossing that brotherhood around. He leased out the arcades to the shops out front, so they brought in a little income. He insisted on finishing the public spaces and theater first, so they could start showing movies even before the rest of the place was finished."

"Is it all done now?" Gayle asked. "Or are you going to fix up the back halls and dressing rooms, too? Not that there's anything wrong with them now," she hastened to add. "I just wondered."

"Not yet," he said. "Most of the public areas were finished, but we still had to put a lot of money into the place before we could open the theater. In the end, my grandfather bought out the whole place. He said it was cheaper than continuing in business with the brotherhood."

"You spent a lot of money on art," Gayle said.

"Some of it came from home," he said, "but some of it was purchased for the Empire. Not everything was expensive. It was just things I liked." His face clouded. "I have to rearrange most of it. Some items have been stolen, and some are damaged. I'm sure it was mostly guests and not the housekeeping department, but Ernie didn't like the responsibility of dusting them, and she was always grumbling about the girls we hired to help her. She claimed they were too clumsy to be trusted with expensive, fragile things."

"I heard her say that the day I arrived," Gayle said. "She scolded Mr. Langdon at length."

"I doubt Langdon put much thought into the hiring of the cleaning women." John rubbed the back of his neck. "I'm glad I'm not in charge of personnel. Miss Fisher told me yesterday that one of the women came to her office, crying and telling her a story about breaking a small statue. The one of Nefertiti, in the alcove to the left at the top of the first landing. The girl said she told Ernie about it, and Ernie fired her. But then Ernie was killed, and the girl just stayed on. She switched the statue with the one on the other side, so the damaged part couldn't be seen."

"Oh, no. It was good she came to confess!"

"That's the strange part," John said. "A few weeks ago, Miss Fisher actually offered her Ernie's job. Milly ran out of Miss Fisher's office in hysterics, and Miss Fisher hired someone else. Milly says she's been haunted by Ernie's ghost ever since then, and she finally couldn't stand it anymore, so she went to get the statue and bring it to Miss Fisher. When she took Nefertiti from the alcove, it wasn't broken."

"A miraculous healing?" Gayle raised her brows. "That's strange."

"Especially for a heathen statue," he agreed. "The statue is fine. Both statues are fine. Miss Fisher examined them. The girl insisted there was a long crack along on one side of the crown, but Miss Fisher didn't see anything. When I get back to town, I'm going to check the list the insurance man left, to see if it's on there."

"I'm sorry about the thefts," Gayle said. "I know you wanted people to enjoy the artwork. The Empire is still beautiful, though, and you don't need to get rid of everything. You just need to move things so they can't be stolen or broken." Like the marble, which still rested in her bureau drawer among her unmentionables.

"You're right." John straightened. "And now, I'm going to get us something to drink. Do you want to come with me or wait here?"

Gayle bit her lip. This wasn't a date. John should be helping entertain his grandparents' guests.

"I'll just wander around for a while, thank you."

"All right. I'll find you then." He disappeared into the crowd before she could correct the misunderstanding.

Gayle walked the perimeter of the ballroom and stopped at the sight of the Fanshaws talking to John's grandparents. Mrs. Fanshaw was remarkably patient with Lillian. Her friend's sunset-colored frock, with its asymmetrical hem and gold chains where its sleeves ought to be, was a bit much for this formal event. Lillian probably bought it to wear to a nightclub—or to shock her mother-in-law.

If the woman was shocked, she concealed it well. She introduced Lillian to people with the same courtesy she would accord a duchess, smiling and chatting with apparent affection. Lillian's movie star makeup couldn't conceal her genuine pleasure at the party.

"I'm glad you have a friend here." John handed her a glass. "Ginger ale."

"Thank you. Yes, me, too. It was kind of your grandparents to invite me. The music is wonderful."

"Eclectic, anyhow," John said. "I didn't realize your friend —Lillian?—was married to Willie Fanshaw. We were at school together, for a while."

According to Lillian, Willie hadn't stayed at college long. Once he'd realized that classes would interfere with sports and social activities, he'd given up the college classes. After all, he had family money.

"Yes, they were married two weeks ago." She sipped at her ginger ale. Too sweet.

"You said you'd known her all your life?"

Gayle nodded. "Our parents were friends. They all grew up together and then when they moved out to the suburbs, they built houses near each other. Lillian and I were more like sisters than friends."

"That's good. I didn't have any siblings when I was young." He paused. "I mean, I have a younger brother and sister now, from my father's second marriage, but they're kids."

"Lillian had an older brother," Gayle said. "Lillian adored him. He was always kind to us. My older sister was bossy, and she married Michael. We'd known him all our lives, too, and he was just as bossy as she was. Is."

"You're both lucky to have such a good circle of family and friends," he said. "Hey, are you all right? Let's go sit down." He held her elbow and led her to a round table. "You look pale. Did I say something wrong?"

"No, no. I was lucky. Blessed. But Lillian didn't have such a good time of things. It's a long story and not for such a happy occasion as this."

She thought he might press for more information, but after a few seconds he nodded. "Your brother-in-law found the right career, if he's been bossy all his life."

"Oh, yes. He always wanted to be a police officer. And even though I tease him, he's really pretty good at it. He's hoping to get promoted again soon, even though he's only been a sergeant for a year."

"I hope he succeeds," John said. "Is his job dangerous? Chicago's becoming a dangerous place lately, not far from the Empire."

"It was," Gayle said, "before he got promoted. He was always having to assist the Prohibition agents with raids and then the paperwork." She laughed. "He's a very law-abiding citizen, but he's always annoyed with them for arresting people and expecting him to do all the paperwork and getting the criminals—who aren't always real criminals..." She wrinkled her nose. "Well, they are criminals, but they aren't the kind of criminal Michael is used to arresting and putting in jail. Sometimes, they're respectable people. Not violent, even though they're breaking the law by running stills."

"Prohibition is the law," John said. "I don't drink, and neither do my grandparents." He held up his glass of ginger ale. "My father was annoyed when the Volstead Act was passed—not because he drinks, but because of the tax issue. He says he'd rather the government got their money from liquor taxes than taxing him directly."

Gayle laughed. "My father was annoyed with that, too. He's in favor of prohibition, but he says it's immoral to tax a man for working."

"I don't think my father looks at it quite like that," John said. "He just doesn't like giving away his money. Still, it takes a certain amount of money to run a country, and they have to get it somewhere."

"My parents have quite spirited discussions about that," Gayle said. "My mother is an activist, always wanting more government money for her projects, and my father is opposed to the income tax. They both agree with each other's points of view, but they aren't changing their own opinions, either."

John grinned. "Political contention in the home of a respectable Presbyterian minister?"

"Only in the privacy of their own dining room," Gayle said. "My parents adore each other to an embarrassing degree. In public, Mother's an independent, feminist kind of woman. At home, she's always making Papa's favorite meals and keeping everything just the way he likes it."

"It sounds like you have an interesting home," he said. "Here's an empty table."

Gayle sat. "We're all very different. Ruth got married to her childhood sweetheart right after high school and started having babies. My mother had great hopes for me, so I went to junior college with the idea of becoming a teacher. I graduated, but instead of going on to do good works, I took off for New York, to learn how to play the organ for the movies. Dot, who's three years younger than me, is in college now, and she'll be the one to change the world. She doesn't know if she wants to be a social worker, a lawyer, or the President of the Unites States."

"Is she your mother's favorite?" John asked.

"You would think so, but Ruth has produced two grandchildren, and it's hard to compete with that. And before you ask, she's proud of me, too, for doing what I want to do—even if she doesn't understand it. She sometimes mentions other, more prestigious, careers in music, but she doesn't pressure me." Gayle sipped her ginger ale. "She's probably afraid I'll want to become an automobile mechanic next, since I've been talking about my car so much."

"It would be convenient to have a mechanic in the family," he said. "Are you interested in a different career? Just asking as a friend, not as your employer…although I'd hate to lose the city's only lady organist." He grinned. "I didn't know there was a college course in learning to play the organ for films. You just took off for New York on your own? Did your parents approve of that?" He waved at a waiter and waited for the man to change their empty glasses for full ones.

"Well, they didn't like the idea of me going alone, but I'd already finished at the junior college, and Lillian was there. In New York, I mean. They thought it would be good for me to be there."

"For you to be with Lillian?" John looked at the dance floor, where Lillian was kicking up her heels, her brilliant skirt flaring out above her knees.

"Lillian was living with a relative out there." Gayle tucked a strand of hair behind her ear. "The thing is…my parents were worried about her. Her parents…" She sighed. "They died of the Spanish flu when Lillian and I were 16. Lillian, Dot, and I had gone to stay with my aunt and uncle outside of town, because our parents were helping at the hospitals and taking care of sick people. My parents were fine, but hers got sick and died in just a few days. She didn't have a chance to say goodbye, and they couldn't even have a funeral."

John shook his head. "That was a hard time."

"Her grandfather insisted she come to live with him in

New York, especially since my parents were still in the city. So she lost us, too, as well as her parents. She thought her brother would bring her back to Chicago when he got home, but then…" Gayle swallowed. "Jack was killed in the war." She gave him a tight smile. "Not such a long story after all. Just a really sad one."

"Thank you for telling me," John said. "I hope she finds happiness in her marriage."

"Me, too. Her grandfather died and left her a little money, so she came back to live with an aunt in Chicago, and then the aunt wanted to move back to New York…so Lillian has had a rough time of things. I hope Willie makes her happy, and she settles down."

John looked at them. "I don't know him well, but the Fanshaws have a reputation for being generous and kind. And she has a good friend in you. Would you like to go outside and look at the lake?"

Gayle jumped to her feet. "Yes, I would. It's such a beautiful lake, and the moonlight made endless ripples on it last night. I want to store up the images before we go back to the city."

"We have Lake Michigan there," he said. "That's beautiful, too, and bigger."

"I know. It's just not the same as the lake with the trees all around it. Lillian and I took the train out here and then the water taxi from the station to the Fanshaws' house. It's beautiful on the water. All of the houses—even the biggest mansions—are set back from the edge of the lake, so it still looks natural."

"I would have driven you up in my car." He took her arm. "Both of you, so you didn't have to take the train."

"We traveled first class," Gayle said. "It was quite comfortable and clean, and I wanted to take the water taxi. Mrs. Fanshaw and Willie both have cars here, so we didn't need a third."

He held the door open for her, and they stepped into the cool evening. The sunset was glorious all around them, casting a tail of fire over the surface of the water.

"Have you ever been here before?" John asked.

"When we were younger, Lillian and I came here for summer camp." She pointed to the west side of the lake. "Over there, somewhere. We came twice—no, three times. Lots of mosquitoes, and it rained, but we went swimming and boating nearly every day. There were horses to ride, too, which made us feel very dashing, but they were probably very dull animals, in real life, if they let schoolgirls ride them. We played games and sang songs around a campfire. I won all the sports, and Lillian always won the prize for scripture memorization."

John cast an involuntary glance toward the hotel, and Gayle laughed. "Yes, she did. There's more to Lillian than most people see."

"I've always liked it here," John said. "I never went to any kind of camp, but my grandparents let me bring my friends here. It made me popular." He lifted his head. "They're playing a foxtrot. Would you like to dance?"

"I would like that."

He extended his arm, and she took it, pushing away the idea that the gesture was too intimate. He was just being polite.

The foxtrot was less physical than the Charleston, but they finished the dance with laughter, breathing quickly.

"You're a good dancer," Gayle said.

"So are you! I'm curious. How did a minister's daughter get to be such a light-footed hoofer? Were you hanging out in clubs in New York? Speakeasies?" His voice was warm and teasing, but Gayle blushed. She hoped her color would be attributed to the energetic dance.

"School was expensive," she said. "I played piano at some of the dance halls there in New York. Nothing like what you're thinking of. These were legal and respectable. I even played in a few here in Chicago, but…" She sat in the chair he pulled out for her. "My father doesn't find dancing—at least, most dancing—immoral, but some of his parishioners do. Even if they don't, they might not approve of his daughter working at a dance hall. I got the job at the Empire soon after we returned from New York, so I didn't have to look for anything else."

"We? I thought you went out there alone," John said.

"Lillian came back with me." Gayle accepted another glass of ginger ale. She didn't want to talk about Lillian. "Where did you go to school? What course of study did you take?"

"Business, of course, since my grandfather was paying for it. He said I'd need to know business, whatever I decided to do with my life. I went to Northwestern, came home, lounged around in his office for a while and then he set me up with the Empire." He grinned. "Sometimes it's a big responsibility, especially lately, but it's still a very fun place."

"You get to watch all the shows you want," Gayle said. "What are your favorites?"

"I'm afraid I have very childish tastes." John leaned back in the small chair. "I like movies with adventure. Mysteries, too, but mostly the exciting movies. Books, too. *Terror Island* and *Haldane of the Secret Service*. You probably have more sophisticated tastes."

"I've played the church organ since I was twelve years old, and I'm now accompanying movies and vaudeville acts," Gayle said. "The adventurous films are more fun than the dramas. I do still play at church, too, of course."

"Of course," he agreed. "It is a well-rounded repertoire."

Golda Levine approached their table. She glowed, pink cheeks owing nothing to rouge. "I saw you dancing. I'm so glad."

"Thank you for inviting me," Gayle said. "The supper was delicious, and the music is excellent."

"I told them what to play," Golda said complacently, "and they are doing a fine job. I like the jazz music, but Abraham… he likes other things better."

"Your dress is lovely," Gayle said.

"Thank you." Golda lifted an arm to admire the lace shawl. "At my age, a dress with no sleeves and no back…it's not a good idea. I like the new dresses, but not all of them." Her silver crown gleamed in its nest of white hair. "I feel like a bride in this, if not a young one." She leaned toward Gayle and whispered, "Abraham likes it, too."

"I am sure he does."

Golda turned to John. "Your grandfather needs you to make a speech now, and then some of these people will leave. It is so crowded here."

"You wanted a big party," John said.

"Yes, and I had it, and now I want some quiet." Golda smiled at Gayle again. "I hope you will stay, of course."

FIFTEEN

Just when she'd begun to think the weather was improving, it came back like a lion. The wind caught Gayle's umbrella, and she fought to keep it from turning inside out. It might be better to shut it up and get wet than to wrestle with the umbrella and risk breaking it. Suddenly, the wind wrenched the umbrella from her grasp. She collided with a man as she grasped at it. He grunted and stepped back, and she caught the umbrella before it fell in the gutter.

"I'm so sorry, sir. Are you all right?" Gayle grimaced when she recognized the man. "Mr. Bennet. I'm sorry. My umbrella got away from me, and I didn't want to lose it."

He scowled at her. "Quite all right. If you'll excuse me…"

"Hey, Mr. Bennet!" A boy ran from the hotel, waving a glove. "You dropped this in the elevator." He loitered after handing it over, and Bennet dug in his pocket for change. The boy lifted his hat and ran back into the hotel, obviously considering the wetting worth the tip.

Rain dripped off Bennet's nose, and Gayle felt a little guilty about not offering to share her umbrella. It would have been awkward, though, and she was—if she was honest—not inclined to do it.

"I'll see you inside, then." Gayle hurried across Clover street and into the theater. Mr. Starek must pay his staff well, if they frequented the Halstead House. Michael said Mr. Langdon had an apartment in an expensive hotel. The Halstead would have been convenient for him. Maybe Mr. Bennet lived there, too.

Gayle headed for the musicians' lounge, nodding at a passing member of the vaudeville troupe. The girl looked pretty and natural without her heavy stage makeup. What was her life like, moving on the train from city to city, playing in new theaters every few weeks? It might be fun for a while, especially if you were with your family or a group of friends. It would get lonely to not have a home, though.

The musicians' lounge was crowded, with the orchestra members huddled around the piano in animated conversation. Art Hadley looked up and nudged his companions. They stopped talking and regarded her curiously.

"Hello." She smiled. Some of them nodded. Others lifted a hand in greeting. A few murmured a response. None of them came close or engaged her in conversation. She persevered. "Terrible weather today."

"Supposed to rain all week," Chester Klee said. He seemed embarrassed by the words and slid out the door.

Exasperated, Gayle surveyed the rest of them. They drifted back to their conversation around the piano, quieter this time, and she had a feeling they'd changed the topic. She turned and walked to the locker room, glad she didn't rely on her coworkers for her social life.

SIXTEEN

The insurance man dropped a list on John's desk and sat, without invitation, in the guest chair. "You are missing all of these items," he said, "and I am afraid we will decline payment."

John snatched up the list and scanned it. "Not all of these." He pointed. "This one I took home, and this one is at the restorers." He winced. "Someone knocked it off the wall."

With exaggerated patience, the man pulled a pen from his pocket and drew a line through the items. "All of these items had inadequate security precautions. I regret to inform you that my company has instructed me to inform you that we are canceling your policy forthwith."

"You can't do that!" John stared at him. "I'll move things. Set up new security."

"In the course of my inventory," the man said, "I found at least a dozen items that were not listed with our company. Perhaps you already have another insurer?"

"Um, no." John scanned the paper, running a finger down the list. He stopped at an entry and looked up, horrified. "The Louis Comfort Favrile vase?"

"I found no sign of it."

"It was in the Seraglio Ballroom," John said, "on a pedestal near the piano. It wouldn't have been easy to steal. It's at least sixteen inches tall, and that room is only used for special events, not open to the public."

"It might not have been a guest," the man said. "You have caterers and workmen in here every day, preparing for events, carrying crates and boxes. It would have been simple to set it into a box and carry it outside in broad daylight. Your staff members—especially the housekeepers and maintenance department—wander around without supervision."

"Oh, I don't think my employees would steal from me," John said. "I pay them adequate wages and treat them well."

"You don't pay as well as Louis Comfort." The man jabbed toward the list. "Most of those things could be picked up and put in a lady's purse or under a coat. With thousands of people in and out of here every day, it's irresponsible to have anything of value—anything portable—in easy reach." He stood. "I could only inventory those items listed with us. You have quite a few other things of value out there, so you may be missing items we are unaware of."

"I've just added a few things here and there," John pleaded. "I'd be glad to rearrange things and make them more secure." His grandfather would kill him if he lost the insurance. He'd be more upset about that than the missing artwork.

"I'll talk to my supervisor." He didn't sound encouraging. "We cannot accept responsibility under these circumstances."

John stood and hurried around the desk to accompany him to the door. "Oh—I meant to ask you…the two Nefertiti busts on the upper-level balcony. Those were all right, weren't they?"

"I did see them," the man said, "but they weren't listed on your policy. I assumed you only insured the genuine items, not the reproductions."

John frowned. "They're not genuine from a 3000-year-old

tomb, but they were made in Egypt about 200 years ago. I'm fairly sure I added them to the inventory."

"Not with us. The ones I saw on the balcony weren't anywhere near 200 years old, either. I hope you didn't pay much for them." He stepped into the hallway. "You'll be getting a letter in the mail."

"Wait," John said. "Have your supervisor call me. Even if you don't want to insure the contents of the theater, we'd like to keep the rest of the policy. The liability and fire insurance." They insured the entire theater, which was still partly owned by his grandfather's bank, and as much as he'd rather not think about it, theaters were vulnerable to fire. Already this year, two of the largest movie palaces in Chicago had burned down. He had to have insurance.

SEVENTEEN

If the matinees got any longer, they'd run right into the evening shows. Gayle stretched her neck in a circle before rising from the bench. The new band wasn't nearly as good as the Ingenues, relying more on their personal attributes than their musical talents for their applause. So, Mr. Bennet had instructed her to add another short solo at the end of the show.

She passed through the empty lounge, wrinkling her nose. The windowless room, lit only by the lamp in the hallway, was dark and stuffy, with cigarette smoke embedded in the furnishings. Gayle loathed the smell. It stained the walls and windows, too. What was it doing to the insides of the human body?

The locker room was a little better. It hadn't taken Gayle long to realize she didn't want to travel to and from the theater in her performance gowns, so she'd developed a routine. She'd have to make it quick today, or she'd miss the streetcar. She locked the door and removed her makeup before changing into her street clothes. She could easily fold up her thin dress and tuck it into her portfolio bag. Soon, she'd be able to drive herself to work and home again, not having to rush for the streetcar. She draped her scarf around her neck and pulled on her hat with less reverence than the beaded cloche deserved.

She tugged her portfolio from the locker and dropped it, unprepared for its weight and bulk. Puzzled, Gayle set the bag on a chair and opened it, gasping at a spark of light inside. She lifted out a black and silver beaded lamp. She'd never seen it before. The lamp was designed to be artistic rather than functional, and she knew it must be valuable.

She caught her breath, frightened. Were those footsteps in the hallway? Gayle opened the locker next to hers and stuffed the lamp inside, behind a coat. Instantly, she pulled it out again. She didn't want someone else blamed.

Without regard for wrinkles, Gayle stuffed her dress into the portfolio bag, unlocked the door and slid into the dark lounge, clutching the lamp. The voices in the hall grew louder. She set the lamp on a small table between two armchairs. It would blend in with all the litter there: a bigger lamp, two ashtrays, a stack of newspapers, and three empty coffee cups. Heart thumping, she was on her way out the door when Bennet appeared.

He frowned—his usual expression whenever he saw her—and stepped into the room, followed by Chester Klee. Klee turned on the light by the door and stood in the entrance. "I thought you said Jesse would be here."

Gayle was devoutly glad he wasn't. "I haven't seen him."

"You said to meet you in the rehearsal hall," Jesse said from behind him. "I waited there for ten minutes."

"I said the lounge," Bennet snapped. "You were supposed to be here."

Jesse glanced at his watch. "Well, you're ten minutes late, anyhow."

"What were you doing here in the dark?" Klee asked Gayle.

She nearly melted under their scrutiny, acutely aware of the lamp in the far corner of the room. "Just leaving. I need to go, or I'll miss the streetcar." She smiled brightly. "I'm saving for a car, you know. Then, I won't have to rush off." She had to stop babbling like an idiot. "Goodbye."

"Cars are expensive," Klee said.

Jesse slid around him into the lounge. "How much money does a lady organist make?"

Annoyance made her forget the current danger. "That's none of your business. I've been saving for a long time, and I do other jobs, too." She bit her tongue to stop its wagging. That part really was none of their business, as long as it didn't interfere with her work at the Empire.

"That's right." Jesse snapped his fingers. "You performed for the Emperor's family shindig. As a member of the union…"

Gayle cut him off. "I have to go." She pushed past them, ignoring whatever it was that Jesse called after her, practically running by the time she reached the exit.

She rounded the corner of Clover in time to see the streetcar lurch away, and she sagged in disappointment. It would be an hour before the next one, and she didn't want to go back inside. She was hungry, too. She'd have to start bringing a snack, to eat surreptitiously between her parts of the show. The matinee performances took over three hours, from start to finish, plus the time it took her to set up and get out again. The theatergoers probably ate an early lunch first, or they went out to dinner right after the show. Maybe she could bring a lunch and eat it in the lounge before the show, or a sandwich for afterward, instead of having to wait until she got home.

Trying to think about food was futile; Gayle couldn't get her mind off the lamp. How could it have ended up in her locker? Maybe someone had put it in there, afraid to get caught with it, just as she had almost done to the person whose locker was next to hers. She sent up a heartfelt prayer of gratitude for the misunderstanding that sent Jesse to the wrong room. If he'd been there when she found the lamp… She shivered and repeated the prayer.

She couldn't have explained it away, and her honest protests of innocence would have been unconvincing. She'd have to talk to Michael. He'd believe her. He'd listened to her story about the orb, and this was more of the same, on a larger scale. He'd called the orb a bit of mischief, but this was an expensive lamp, not a little item that would sit unnoticed in her pocket.

Gayle turned in a circle. She couldn't stay here, outside the theater, afraid that the men would find the lamp and come out to accuse her. If she walked for a while, along the streetcar line, she could catch it a few blocks further on. She set out, walking too fast at first, catching the attention of passersby, and forced herself to slow to a more casual stroll. She shouldn't feel so guilty.

Another idea struck her—one so shocking that Gayle stopped. She stumbled forward again, propelled by the man behind her.

"Sorry," he said. "Are you all right?"

"It was my fault," she said. "I'm fine."

He nodded, obviously in agreement, and stepped around her. She watched him go. Why had he been following so closely? Was she being paranoid? He looked like a perfectly normal man—not a police officer or a criminal.

And why would either of those follow her? Gayle set out again, walking more slowly, forcing herself to face the truth: someone had put that lamp in her locker intentionally, not just to upset her, but actually expecting her to be found with it. If the show hadn't lasted so long, there would have been orchestra members around.

She realized she'd slowed to a stop again. People walked around her as she concentrated. Who could have done that? Jesse? He would love to get her in trouble, just out of spite, but would he go so far as to involve her in a crime? He might want her fired and replaced, but did he hate her enough to do something that might get her sent to jail?

She started walking again, propelled by a desire to set as much space as possible between herself and the theater. The blare of a car horn made her jump, twisting around in panic.

A blue Kissel Gold Bug pulled to the curb, John Starek at the wheel. He waved and smiled, and she did her best to provide an appropriate response before continuing her walk. He hit the horn again and called her name. She stopped.

He pulled the car forward, even with her. "You're in a hurry. Can I give you a ride somewhere?"

That would be awful. "No, thank you," Gayle said. "I'm catching the streetcar just up there." She pointed in the general direction. "It's been a long day."

"Let me take you home, then," he said. "I can get you there faster than a streetcar."

The understatement made her chuckle in spite of the situation. "I'm sure you could, but I don't mind taking the streetcar."

"And you do object to riding with me?" he asked.

His grin made it a teasing question, but Gayle wasn't reassured. Her empty stomach hurt.

"Come on, get in." He reached over and pushed open the door. "I won't bite, and I'll drive carefully."

She stood, unable to extricate herself from the situation. She wanted to reach the safe haven of her home, but she was too confused and worried to be a casual companion. Still, she couldn't refuse for any valid reason. Besides, it was a Gold Bug.

She stepped into the street, carefully avoiding a pile of manure. Automobiles made less of a mess than horses in traffic, she thought idly as she slid onto the leather seat, and they were more exciting. This one was the best she'd ever seen, and she was actually riding in it!

"Where do you live?" he asked. "Do you really need to go straight home? Would you let me buy you dinner first?"

That wouldn't work, even if she weren't in such a muddle. Gayle shook her head. "No, thank you."

He winced. "Because you don't like me or because I'm your boss?"

How was she supposed to answer that? Before she could come up with something, he laughed ruefully. "I'm sorry. That was inappropriate. I'm feeling a little battered after a lecture from my grandfather and feeling sorry for myself. If you could tell me you think I'm intelligent and sensible, I'd be very appreciative."

She laughed. "You are intelligent and sensible."

"Hm." He appeared to consider. "Thanks. I'm not sure it helped, but it was kind of you." He glanced in the mirror before entering the road again.

"Not at all. It's true."

"And I'm a responsible business owner?" He glanced at her. "I don't suppose you could say that, too?"

"Well," she said, "I don't have any reason to think otherwise." Her anxiety was fading under his charm. She rested against the cushion. "Did someone say you aren't?"

"My grandfather's unhappy with me. He thinks I should have been more responsible with the valuable things at the theater." He blew out a long breath. "He's right. Things have been broken, and now the insurance company is refusing to cover some thefts. Quite a few thefts."

Gayle froze. Thefts?

"I wasn't even going to file a claim," he said, "but they want to cancel the policy altogether. That would be fine with me. The adjuster was an obnoxious man. We could find another insurance company. But my grandfather wasn't happy."

"No, I suppose not." She sounded a little strangled. Gayle

swallowed and tried again. "Insurance is important, isn't it? With so many theaters burning down all the time?"

"We're very careful at the Empire, but it's always a danger." John returned to his complaint. "The worst part is that he blames me for the thefts—not that I stole anything, as the adjuster implied, but because I made it an irresistible temptation to people."

"Oh." Gayle considered that. "But that doesn't make it your fault."

"He says it does, because as the owner, I'm ultimately responsible for these kinds of things. This was something I could have prevented." After a pause, he looked over at her. "Aren't you going to try to reassure me?"

She smiled. "Could I? It sounds to me like you already know he's right."

He gave her a mock scowl. "I should have let you take the streetcar."

She wanted to laugh. Wanted to cry. Mostly, she wished he had, indeed, let her take the streetcar.

EIGHTEEN

"In general," Bennet said, "your playing is fine. Very good. Your stage presence, unfortunately, is still...weak. Modesty is a fine characteristic in a church organist, but if you're going to succeed here, you need more panache. More style."

He wanted her to rehearse style? Gayle wished Lillian were there to laugh at the idea. How did one practice panache? She nodded and tried to look confident. After finding the lamp in her bag, she had no confidence at all. She certainly didn't have the kind of attitude required for celebrity. Couldn't people admire her skill unless she looked and acted like an actress? Or was that kind of respect only found in the highbrow atmosphere of classical music?

"I got new dresses and makeup," Gayle said. He'd told her to come in for a rehearsal, so he must not be planning to fire her. She tried to focus on his words and not think about the lamp.

"Yes, you look fine." Bennet twisted his arm to look at his watch. "I want you to go through tomorrow's show. Smile." He waved his hand. "Act it out. Stand up and bow."

Was he joking? Did he plan to stand there and watch her like a stage director?

"It's always hard for me to know when to stand and bow." *Or how to do it without feeling like an idiot,* she thought. "At school, they said to do it at the end of the performance and to keep it short." Gayle felt her stomach muscles tighten. "But I'm willing to learn."

Jesse made his whole performance a…well, a performance. His personality—touched with more than a little arrogance—lent itself to that kind of thing. Gayle didn't know if she could pull it off. She'd expected theater music to be more fun than the orchestra or church music. Definitely more fun than teaching music classes to children. Instead, it was stressful.

"You don't learn style in school," Bennet said, "and Eastman's program is a sham."

"A sham?" Gayle scowled. "It's not a sham. I learned a lot from that course, and it was taught by some fine teachers—experienced theater organists, including Rosa Rio, who is a well-respected female organist."

Bennet shrugged. "If you say so, but there's more than technical playing to theater performance. Watch Jesse and Mr. Shores."

Gayle compressed her lips. Now, he was suggesting that even Mr. Shores was better than she was. He was more experienced, of course—just at a different theater. "I'll work on it."

"Good." He picked up a newspaper, shook it out, and settled in the chair behind her. "Wilkes isn't available, so just play the score straight through."

How could she give a dramatic interpretation of the film without seeing it? She stared at Bennet for a few seconds, certain that he was smirking at her behind the shield of the newspaper. Why did he dislike her? It wasn't just prejudice against women. Gayle was sure of it.

Lillian may have coerced Mr. Langdon into giving her the

job, so she could understand his hostility—if he'd been around to display any—but why would Mr. Bennet feel that way?

She turned around and prepared to play. "Do you want the riser music and solo pieces?"

"No, just the score."

That didn't make sense at all. If she were lacking flamboyance, those would have been the problem areas. Once she embarked on the movie accompaniment, she was just background. She shouldn't be drawing attention to herself at all.

"Play it straight through, just as it's written. There's no need for improvisation with this score."

She tried to imagine the movie as she played. She'd only seen it twice. A few minutes into the performance, he interrupted.

"Too slow. Start over."

She took a deep breath. She was not going to argue with him, to give him reason to fire her, and she wouldn't be harassed into quitting. Wordlessly, she turned the pages back to the beginning and started over. The timing had felt right.

He let her play the first two scenes—over half an hour—without interruption, but when she began the piece designated for the intermission, he said, "Stand up and bow."

She felt ridiculous, bowing to the right and left in an empty room. He sat, newspaper on his lap, head tipped to one side. "Smile and wave. Not a big wave. Just like this." He set the newspaper on the table and stood, gesturing. "Friendly, but not too casual."

Jesse always bowed with a flourish, but he was a man, bowing dramatically from the waist. She would look silly trying that. She tried again, and apparently it was acceptable, because Bennet dropped back into the chair.

She finished the intermission music, feeling his eyes on her as she played. She stood and waved, smiling and bowing.

Could she possibly finish this idiotic rehearsal before the

evening show? Mr. Bennet would have to be backstage soon, supervising and criticizing the new musical act as they prepared for their Empire debut.

As if he read her mind, he said, "Play the next scene. It's nearly five o'clock, and we need to get ready for the show. I assume you're able to stay and watch Jesse perform tonight?"

Resigned, she nodded. "Of course."

Midway through the next scene, he interrupted her. "It's five twenty. Collect your belongings and follow me."

Confused, Gayle obeyed, holding her portfolio bag securely as she trailed behind him through the halls. He turned, when they were backstage, looking around as if seeking someone. "I want to introduce you to the Splendid Belles. They're the new musical act, and you should consult with them to see what they want for introduction or closing."

She'd never done any such thing. Normally, he gave her those instructions. Before they found the women he was looking for, he hailed the maintenance department head. "Moe! Wait up. I want a word with you." He looked back at Gayle. "Never mind. Just watch what Jesse does. It's nearly six o'clock now. You'd better be seated."

Gayle checked her own watch. Five thirty. She'd have time to freshen up and reach the box reserved for theater people and special guests. She hadn't played this film yet—only watched it in the rehearsal room—and in spite of her irritation, she'd be glad of the opportunity to relax and enjoy the performance.

Just before six, she slipped into the box, still clutching her portfolio.

"Hello there!"

To her surprise, John sat in the box. He stood and waited for her to sit—an old-fashioned courtesy that charmed her. She smiled up at him. "I've been ordered to watch and learn."

He chuckled. "Well, you can enjoy the show at the same time, can't you? The illusionist may be better tonight."

"You have a new all-girl band, too," she said. "They seem to be popular."

"The agency sends them—or rather, sends a list for us to approve or reject. They're under new management in the past few months, I understand, which might account for the illusionist. They're usually pretty good at picking winners. The vaudeville troupes are on a circuit, so we don't have a lot of choice with them. We'll be getting a new troupe next week. This one has a dog."

"A dog?" Gayle asked. "A real dog? I hope it's well-trained."

"Me, too, and I hope it's a hit. They're usually not. We're supposed to be getting quality acts, not freak shows. The new management might be falling down on that," John said. "Most of the shows have been fine, but we don't usually get dogs."

"Are you getting Helen Keller? My sister wants to see her."

John scratched his ear. "I hate to crush your good opinion of me, but my tastes run to the entertaining and frivolous. I saw that act once. It was quite informative and more political than I'd expected."

"Political?"

"And boring, at least to me. She's been on the circuit for years, so people must like her."

"I didn't think it sounded very interesting, either," Gayle admitted, "but it probably ought to be. Dot and my mother thought her vaudeville shows were demeaning. They said she shouldn't be on the same stage as performing dogs."

That made him chuckle. "I enjoy the dogs, and I'm not highbrow enough for the intellectual acts. I'm sure she does good, so it's nothing personal. I don't know why she'd want to do the circuits anyhow, unless she needs the money."

"Maybe she does," Gayle said. She looked around the theater with satisfaction. "This is the best seat in the house. Look at all those happy people."

Women in brightly colored dresses and pretty caps

laughed and chatted with each other. They weren't all wealthy women. It was easy for most women to dress well now, with so many department stores. The current fashions were easy to make at home, too—a nice change from the long skirts and fitted bodices of the last decade. So much less fabric, too. Economical. Gayle smiled at the thought.

John looked fine tonight, too, in black and white, and Gayle felt pretty and comfortable with a clean face and her Nile green dress. It wasn't a date. It was just…being in the same place at the same time, all dressed up. Of course, everyone dressed up to go to the Empire. And here she was, with the Emperor.

"That's a nice smile," he said. "A penny for your thoughts."

"They aren't worth a penny," Gayle said. "I was just thinking about the audience, and how everyone dresses up to come here."

He gazed over the audience with patent satisfaction. "They're having a grand time, aren't they? Everyone is glad to be out, enjoying the music and the shows. I like making people happy."

"Then you're in the right business. The vaudeville shows make them laugh," Gayle said.

"The laughter is the best. You sure look pretty tonight."

The unexpected compliment warmed her cheeks. He liked this look better than when she was all made up for the shows? "Thank you." She tucked a strand of hair behind her ear and tried to think of something else to say.

"It's late, isn't it?" John consulted his watch. On cue, the ceiling began its transformation to a night sky.

Gayle squinted into the dark pit. "I don't even see him."

John leaned forward. "I think he's there. It looks like he's getting the music set up or something. I can see light reflecting off his hair."

Gayle giggled. Twenty-five was too old to giggle, and it

was wrong to make fun of Jesse, but she was having such a good time she couldn't resist. John was good company.

"I hope he's ready," she said, "because Mr. Wilkes is going to flip that switch at any second. Jesse would hate to be caught unprepared."

As if on cue, the organ started rising. The music didn't. Gayle's smile faded as she stared at the man hunched over the emerging organ. Jesse's head rested on the top manual, arms dangling at his sides. Was he sick?

Illuminated by the spotlights, he looked unconscious. Maybe…

John stood and headed for the door. "Come on. No, head up to the projection room and tell them to lower the organ. I'll telephone the police."

"The police?"

"Then I'll meet him…the organ in the basement." John called the last few words over his shoulder. He stopped and turned back. "No, you call the police as soon as you get them to lower the organ. I'd better go down there right away. He might not be dead yet."

Not dead yet. Gayle took a deep breath, shocked by the sudden change in their evening. "Why call the police?"

"Didn't you see it in the spotlight? There was blood in his hair. It had run down onto his white collar."

He took off at a sprint toward the side stairs, and Gayle hastened in the other direction. The riser music was normally played while people were still settling into their seats. It signaled the start of the show, but no one paid much attention to it until the music changed from the riser music to the start of the solo. The audience was starting to notice now. A wave of confusion swept over the theater, with an increasing sense of alarm.

NINETEEN

The orchestra rose from its pit to stage level, playing a jazzy tune as John reached the organ. Bennet was in the basement, pale, punching the button to lower the organ, which was already sitting on the basement floor. The gears ground, and John pushed his hand away.

Even in the basement, the organ—and Jesse—could be seen from some of the seats. John looked around.

"Can we close up the stage floor from here?"

Flustered, Bennet pushed another button. The organ began to rise, and he jabbed at the button to lower it again. "This one."

With the buzz from the audience muffled by the door, John leaned over Jesse, trying to see if the man was alive. He had to be alive. Another member of the Empire killed—and the blood on the back of the man's head did indicate a murder—would be awful.

JOHN SPENT the next hour in a ghastly daze. Fortunately, the police hadn't wanted to detain three thousand theatergoers.

They'd not even objected to the show continuing, as long as the organ wasn't disturbed. Possibly, they didn't want a mob of upset and curious people interfering with their investigation.

Bennet had made a brief announcement that the organist had fallen ill, but the show would go on. The show must go on. At one point, John realized that Bennet was playing the piano to accompany the film. The vaudeville acts performed and elicited their usual laughter. No one realized that the room below their seats was full of policemen. It had taken the doctor only a few minutes to pronounce death, probably caused by a blow with a blunt instrument. Again, John thought, the blunt instrument, but there were no convenient statues in the basement.

The police were more serious and organized this time. This wasn't the odd death of a cleaning lady. Jesse Erwin had been a celebrity. And, of course, it was the second murder in two months at the Empire. John sat on a crate and dropped his head into his hands. What was going on? He'd have to close the theater before anyone else was hurt. Killed.

"Mr. Starek."

John looked up to see Michael Brady standing over him. "Sorry. What can I do?"

"We'd like to interview all the musicians and other performers after the show, but in the meantime, can you tell me where your maintenance man is? And anyone else who's likely to be in this area or know that Mr. Erwin would be here at this time?"

"Maintenance," John repeated. "That would be Moe Rogg. He might be gone now, but he has a few men under him, and there's always someone here during the shows, in case anything goes wrong." He broke off, glancing toward the organ room. "His office is by the carpenter's shop, but I wouldn't think he'd be there now." He searched the crowded hall and pointed. "There. That's Rogg. The bald man. You might want to talk to the stagehands, too. They're all over the place before a show."

The police officer made a notation in his book. "Stagehands. What about the orchestra? Wouldn't they have seen him?"

"I don't know," John said. "They might, if they got up and walked around to the doorway, but I don't know. They would have been preparing to go up, too, and the organ platform is a little higher than the orchestra one. It's kept pretty dark, too."

"Detective Ashe will want to speak with you in a few minutes, sir. Would you prefer to do that in your office?"

"Yes," John said, "please. And Miss Wells. She was with me in the box when we saw…Mr. Erwin. Do you know where she is now?"

"With you in a box?" The policeman lowered his brows.

"A reserved box seat, for staff and guests to watch the show. Bennet wanted her to watch Jesse Erwin…" his eyes strayed toward the body, which hadn't yet been moved. "He wanted her to watch the show."

Brady scowled. "And you joined her?"

"No, I was already there to watch the show. I didn't expect her," John said. "Can you tell me where she is now?"

"She's staying with the manager," Brady said. "The woman was upset."

"Miss Fisher?" John asked. "She was upset?"

"In hysterics."

"No," John said. "Miss Fisher was in hysterics? About Jesse?"

Brady shrugged. "Gayle had her under control by the time we left her there. Got her some hot tea. The women of the Wells family think hot tea can cure anything."

"Can I go see her? Both of them?" Gayle was probably fine, but he couldn't picture Miss Fisher in hysterics. On the other hand, she was the theater manager and probably felt responsible. She was new at the job, too, and still proving herself. When the police were here before, she'd said something about how well everything had been going until Ernie and Henry Glassman died. Another death might have been too much for her to handle.

Brady shook his head. "If you would like to leave, you can go to your office. Detective Ashe will be there shortly. We'd prefer that you don't talk to anyone until then."

John stood, averting his eyes from the doorway to the organ room, where men were lowering Jesse's body onto a stretcher. They wanted to get him removed before theatergoers started filling the hallways and street outside.

He climbed the concrete stairs and traversed the long hall to the carpeted steps. For once, the extravagant decor failed to interest him. A few guests loitered in the lobby, casting interested looks at him and whispering as he passed by. The Emperor.

John glanced at the closed door of the manager's office and then up at the chandelier over the stairs, thinking of Ernie, wondering how she had managed to dust it. As he climbed to the mezzanine level and walked to his own office, he was tempted to turn back and check on the women, regardless of the detective's request. His staff was his responsibility. He could telephone, but Ashe wouldn't like that, either.

His secretary was gone, of course. The office was silent, cushioned with drapery, carpet, and upholstery. They absorbed the small noises he made, and the heavy door prevented him from hearing anything from outside. He rose and opened it again. Prowling the large room, he ended up in front of the fireplace and bookshelves. He did read books, sometimes, but these were all brand new, ordered by the designer to lend atmosphere to the room. They were props.

He had a Bible, though. He didn't read it often, but it wasn't entirely untouched, as the others were. John pulled it from the bottom shelf and thumbed through the thin pages. The Old Testament had a lot of murder—more than he wanted to read, under the circumstances, but Psalms might be comforting. Not necessarily the ones about crushing one's enemies beneath one's feet, but some were good.

The book fell open in his hands, to the sixth chapter of Matthew: *Lay not up for yourselves treasures upon earth, where moth and rust doth corrupt, and where thieves break through and steal.*

He slapped the book shut and returned it to the shelf. He'd never expected this kind of mess. It was supposed to be fun. The theater was a grand gift, and John had treated it like an adventure. Most of the infrastructure was already in place, if a bit of a mess. He'd hired Langdon and left it to him and Miss Fisher to do the real work, and he'd devoted himself to make it all beautiful and enjoyable.

He'd made sure the Empire paid decent wages but hadn't given further thought to being responsible for employees and their livelihoods. He had a manager for that. But two dead employees, murdered…and probably murdered by someone here at the theater. Shouldn't he be doing something?

If the police were right about Glassman, this was the second organist to be killed. John started. Gayle. Gayle was an organist. Was she in danger? They had no idea why the other organists were killed, so they should protect Gayle. He picked up his phone and telephoned the manager's office.

"Miss Fisher here." The manager's voice was calm, so the tea must have worked.

"John Starek here. I'm looking for Miss Wells. Is she with you?"

"No, a policeman came for her," Miss Fisher said, "and she left with him."

Maybe Michael Brady had the same concerns John did. "Was it a big man with red hair?"

"I think so. I really don't remember. Miss Wells seemed to know him."

"Thank you." Belatedly, he asked, "Is there anything I can do for you? Do you need anything?"

"No, sir. Everything is under control. The show's almost over, and we'll get everyone out without a problem. I believe the police would prefer to not have Mr. Erwin's death become public information until they talk to his family."

"Does he have a family?" John's heart sank.

"I believe he has parents, sir." Miss Fisher said it as if she was talking about house pets. "I don't believe they were close."

Gayle twisted her fingers together and then untangled them, folding her hands on her lap in an attempt to look poised.

Detective Ashe rocked back on his heels. "According to the other organist, Martin Shores, you were the only person who had a problem with Mr. Erwin. Everyone else liked him."

Suddenly light-headed, Gayle took a deep breath. "I didn't dislike him."

"According to Shores and a few of the other musicians, you were quarreling with him." The detective thumbed over a page of his notebook. "She was very angry with him on several occasions." He turned another page. "You were angry that he hired Mr. Shores to replace you."

"He didn't replace me," Gayle said indignantly. "We needed a third organist."

Detective Ashe shrugged. "It sounds like you were pretty mad."

"Jesse didn't hire Mr. Shores, anyhow. Mr. Bennet hired him." Gayle wished Michael would speak up instead of standing in the background, looking at his feet. "And if I was mad, I got over it."

"According to the theater manager, you felt that Mr. Erwin treated you disrespectfully because of your gender. Is that true?"

"Yes, he did, but I wouldn't kill him over it," Gayle said. "I wouldn't…couldn't do that."

"According to the doctor," the detective said, "you could. The blow was inflicted at an angle, as if you were swinging a baseball bat."

"I don't play baseball, and I didn't do it!" She tried to get control. She'd be in hysterics herself soon.

"Where were you this afternoon?"

Gayle sat up. "I was in the rehearsal hall. Mr. Bennet was with me for at least two hours, and then we went backstage, and then I went to the box seat and John Starek was there. We were together there when we saw the organ rise." Would the man stop hounding her now?

"We'll check all of that, of course," the detective said, "but we're still waiting to find out exactly when Mr. Erwin died. Please don't leave town while we pursue our investigation."

Gayle swallowed, praying the timing would work out right to clear her. She had quarreled with Jesse several times and complained to Miss Fisher about him. It was natural for them to suspect her.

Michael hung back until the other police officers had left. "I'm sorry." He patted her shoulder. "If I utter one word, he'll take me off the case. I don't think he knows about our relationship, and it would be best if he doesn't find out."

"I see." Gayle chewed on her lip. "John Starek knows. I could ask him to not say anything."

"You're not supposed to talk to anyone," Michael said.

"Detective Ashe didn't say that."

"Hm. I wonder if he's having you watched, to see if you do try to talk to anyone." Michael strode toward the door. "I'd better leave. You don't talk to anyone at all. If I get a chance, I'll talk to Starek. You go home."

Gayle grabbed his sleeve. "No, I need to talk to you!"

"What?" Michael shook her off. "Can it wait? Ashe will be looking for me, and I don't want him to see us together."

"It's about…" She took a step back and crossed her arms

across her chest. "You know I went to Lake Geneva to play for Mr. Starek's grandparents' wedding."

He made a rolling motion with his hand, urging her to hurry.

"While I was there, I found three fifty-dollar bills in my bag. The one I carry my music in. One of them fell out when I dropped the bag. Everything spilled out, and John—Mr. Starek—helped me pick it up." The words tumbled out. "He found the first bill. I thought it was his, but he said it wasn't. He said maybe my parents had hidden it in my bag as a surprise."

Michael snorted. "You knew that wasn't true."

"Yes, but I was in a hurry, and he insisted it wasn't his, so I just took it. Then he went away, and when I was straightening out my music, I found two more!"

"Two more?" Michael stared, brows lowered. "What did you do with them?"

She lifted her chin. "I handed them to the pastor after the wedding. I told him I'd found them by the organ—which was true!"

"Well, good. Is that all? Because you could have told me that at home."

"No!" She clutched his sleeve again. "It's not. The other day, when I was leaving, I found a lamp in my bag, in my locker. I'm pretty sure it was a valuable one."

"A lamp? How big is this bag of yours?"

She smacked his arm. "I'm serious, Michael! It was a little beaded lamp with a fringe, like you might put on a nightstand or piano. Even smaller. It had an iron base, with glass and beads on top. Decorative."

He was frowning again. "What did you do with that?"

"I heard people coming, so I stuck it on a table behind some newspapers. I just wanted to get rid of it." She swallowed. "The thing is, Jesse and Mr. Bennet and some of the other musicians arrived just then, and it sounded like Jesse was supposed to be there earlier. If he'd been on time, he would have seen the lamp in my locker."

Michael blew out a breath. "What have you got yourself into?"

"Nothing, I promise!"

"You're certain no one saw you with this lamp?" he asked.

"Yes, and it was gone the next day!"

"Gone?" He lifted his head, listening. "I have to go. Stay out of trouble."

"I really didn't do anything wrong, Michael." Gayle searched his face. Did he believe her? She sounded guilty, even to her own ears.

He grinned and ruffled her hair. "I know that. Go home."

Gayle stepped into the musicians' lounge, wishing Michael were there.

Detective Ashe waved her inside. "Sit down, Miss Wells. We've been talking to Mr. Bennet. He agrees that he was indeed with you all afternoon, but you left after accompanying him backstage. He says you left there about five-thirty. Mr. Starek says you joined him shortly before six o'clock. Can you explain where you were between five-thirty and six?"

"Yes! I came back here, to the dressing room, to freshen up for the show. And I didn't join him there. I just went to the box because Mr. Bennet wanted me to watch the show. I didn't know Mr. Starek would be there."

"Fortunate for you he was," the detective said. "Are you certain you didn't expect him to be there? What would you have done if he weren't?"

"I would have watched the show, and I was expecting to watch Jesse performing!" Gayle was starting to get angry now instead of frightened. It made her feel better. "I didn't kill Jesse."

Bennet crossed his legs, apparently at ease. "Have you had any luck finding Langdon?"

Detective Ashe shook his head. "Are you implying that he had something to do with Erwin's death?"

"I don't see how he could have," Bennet said, "but he does have keys to the theater." He shrugged. "Just wondering."

"Why would Langdon have a reason to kill Erwin?" Ashe asked. "Or the housekeeper or Glassman?"

"No idea. I can tell you one thing, though." Bennet leaned forward in his chair. "I always got the feeling there was something wrong with that man. He was unpredictable. He'd tell me one thing and then deny it the next. Like hiring Miss Wells here. The man's tone deaf. He gave her an audition and then hired her without consulting me or Jesse—at least, not really—even though I'm responsible for the musicians. Then, after she left, he made jokes about it, like he didn't really mean to give her the job. I told him hiring the musicians is my job, and he blew up. Threw a lamp against the wall." Bennet shook his head. "A real loose cannon."

Gayle stared at him. "He did ask you and Jesse! You both said I'd do."

"We couldn't say anything else at that point," Bennet said, "since he was already giving you a rehearsal schedule. Besides, I only had one organist at the time."

The detective rubbed his chin. "Langdon hasn't been seen in nearly two months. Since the day before Miss Ernst died." He turned to look at Gayle.

"Where were you when Miss Ernst died?"

"Me?" She looked at the music director. "Rehearsing, I think."

"Probably." Bennet stood to examine the schedule on the wall, flipping back through the pages. "Yes, I think so. She'd just started, and we were working on a new film. We're so insulated from the rest of theater in the rehearsal hall that it wasn't until we were finished and in the hallway that we realized something was going on."

"But it was right afterward," Gayle said. "Ernie—Miss Ernst—was still there, and Mr. Starek was telling people to call for an ambulance."

"Just as he did last night," Ashe agreed. "When you found Mr. Erwin."

"We didn't find him!" Gayle curled her fingers, digging her nails into her palms. "We just saw him, like everyone else."

"When did he die?" Bennet asked. "Was it right before the show?"

Gayle turned to him, outraged. Was he implying she'd done it after leaving him backstage?

"Mid-afternoon." Ashe consulted his notes. "The coroner says Erwin had been dead for about two hours."

"Two hours!" Gayle sat straighter. "So, you know it wasn't me."

"Not unless the two of you are in collusion." Ashe said. "That seems unlikely, but with the exact same alibi for Miss Ernst, I'm not ignoring the possibility."

"That's ridiculous," Bennet said. "In fact, we weren't the only ones in the rehearsal hall when Ernie was killed."

"So, you do remember the day." Ashe made a note in his book. "Can you tell me who else was there?"

"The projectionist, for one. Up in the booth, but he could see us the whole time."

Gayle nodded, glad to have Bennet's corroboration. It was inconceivable that she might have a motive for killing Ernie, but Ashe didn't seem to be looking for motives—just opportunity.

TWENTY

Lillian stormed into the musicians' lounge as if she belonged there. She glared at the three interested men who were smoking near the window until their smiles faded.

"I need to talk to you. Alone."

Gayle folded up the newspaper, standing before Lillian could demand the men leave. "Let's go for a walk. I have to get ready for the show in about ten minutes, though."

"I'm not sure ten minutes will do it," Lillian said ominously.

"Well, it's all I have. What are you doing here?" She stood aside so Lillian could exit first. "You're not supposed to be wandering around this part of the theater."

"I wasn't wandering. I asked someone where I could find you. Actually, I had to ask three people before someone could tell me, and then they gave me bad directions, so I suppose I was wandering." Lillian waved her hand in a dismissive gesture. "Never mind. You won't believe this, but Willie…" She dropped onto an upholstered bench and stared up at Gayle. "Willie has decided he wants to be a Christian! A Christian! Willie!"

"Oh, Lillian." Gayle's heart swelled and tears sprang to her eyes. "That's wonderful news!"

"It is not wonderful news!" Lillian shouted. "I didn't sign up to marry a Christian!"

"But Lillian, it's a good thing. He'll be a better husband for it." Gayle sat next to her friend. "You're not going to want to party forever, and someday, you'll want to have children. Willie will be a better father as a Christian than as a…." Gayle paused, trying to find a euphemism for describing Willie as a frivolous, foolish young man. "As a sheik." She smiled, hoping her teasing tone would appease her friend. "Was that why he went to see my father?"

"Yes. He said it was a surprise. I couldn't imagine what it was, but I was hoping he'd get to know you and your family like I do."

"Well, if you know and like our family," Gayle said, "and you have known us since you were a baby, you know we're all Christians. So why shouldn't it be okay if Willie is?"

"He'll change everything." Lillian jumped to her feet and paced. "Now that he's got religion, he doesn't want to go out anywhere fun. No more drinking or dancing or good music. He's even trying to give up cigarettes. It's a laugh. I can tell he wants a cigarette or a drink, and it makes him cranky, but he's determined to be saintly about it."

"I can see the smoking and drinking," Gayle said, "but there are respectable places to dance and listen to music. Even the kind of music you like."

"Those are boring."

"I don't think so. Most of your music and dancing are just silly, not immoral."

"I'm not immoral," Lillian said. "I just want to have fun."

Gayle's heart melted at the forlorn comment. She reached out and tugged Lillian back to the bench, putting an arm around her shoulders. "So, have fun. I hope you didn't marry

Willie just on a whim, because it sounded like a fun thing to do, or because he has a lot of money."

"No! He's kind and funny and sweet. He always treated me like a lady, even when we were out in…." She glanced at Gayle from under thick lashes. "Unladylike places. He has good manners."

Gayle grinned. "Well, that's something."

"It's nice," Lillian said. "Not all men do."

"None of those things are inconsistent with being a Christian, Lillian. If anything, they'll be even better, because they'll be coming from a heart that wants to please God. Your father was kind and funny and all those things. He loved you, and you never found him boring, did you?"

"Of course not." Lillian burst into sobs and leaned into Gayle. "I miss him so much."

"Oh, Lillian." Gayle crooned meaningless sounds as her friend cried. When the tears slowed, she sat back. "Willie might become just that kind of man your father was. Not just like him, but Willie with a lot of those good qualities. And you know, your parents would be so glad to know you're married to a Christian man."

"Do you think they do know?" Lillian sniffed. "I don't think they do."

"Of course, they do." Gayle wished her father was here now. "And I know they'd be happy. They'd be even happier if you would turn back to Jesus." Was that right? Could they be sad in Heaven? Gayle decided not to pursue that.

"I can't. I won't."

"You can, Lillian. You know you can. You could do it right now, this very second." Gayle wanted to shake her. She understood why Lillian had rebelled, even if she didn't like it, but couldn't she see that God had just redeemed what might have been a disastrous marriage?

ENGROSSED by the newspaper's review of the new Chalmers coupe, Gayle didn't notice Michael until he cleared his throat. "Miss Wells? Can I have a word with you?"

Gayle set aside the paper and stood, watching her brother-in-law's impassive face, fearful of his news.

"We're leaving." Chester Klee stood. "Come on, Art. Let's leave Miss Wells to be interrogated."

Michael narrowed his eyes at them. "No interrogation. You don't need to leave." He turned back to Gayle. "We're trying to find your friend, Lillian Nagle. Do you know where she might be found?"

She inhaled, trying to calm the butterflies in her stomach. "No, I haven't seen her in a few days. Is she…have you talked to her husband?"

"We haven't been able to locate him, either. His mother says they've gone off on a wedding trip."

"She doesn't know where they went?" Gayle asked. "Are you sure they're actually out of town?"

"Mrs. Fanshaw says they left on Wednesday with suitcases, just saying they were going on a trip and didn't know when they would return."

Gayle bit her lip. "No, Lillian didn't say anything to me. Why do you want to see her?"

Michael glanced at the men. "Just a small matter. Thank you for your time."

Gayle took her seat and picked up the newspaper, but not even the details of the new Thermosyphon cooling system could distract her. Lillian had practically accused Langdon of criminal activity, talking to Jesse at the wedding reception. Now, Langdon was still missing, and Jesse was dead.

She jumped up and started for the door, clutching her portfolio to her chest. "Michael!"

Already at the other end of the hall, he turned and waited for her.

She pulled him through the fire door into the quiet of the

lounge area. "I need to tell you something, Michael. Privately."

He frowned. "About Lillian?"

She nodded. "I don't think I got the job at the Empire because of my credentials. Lillian told me there was an opening, and I thought she'd used her influence to get me an audition. But now…well, I think maybe she pressured Mr. Langdon into actually giving me the job. She knew him in New York. At the wedding reception, she was hinting that he might be using a fake name or have a criminal history or something like that. Jesse Erwin was there."

He held up a hand. "You can't tell me that privately. Not under the circumstances."

"But why are you looking for her? You know she's innocent, and now she's married, and things are getting better for her. I'm sure they are."

"I'm not sure of anything," Michael said, "except that Lillian was gone a long time. I feel sorry for her, but if she's involved in this, Detective Ashe needs to know."

"You can't do that!"

"I can't ignore it. It sounds like exactly the information we need. We still believe Miss Ernst was murdered because she saw something or knew something. Maybe Erwin was killed for the same reason. If Lillian knows something, she'd better tell us before a killer gets to her, too."

"But why are you looking for her?"

"That's police business." Michael scowled, looking much like the sixteen-year-old boy she remembered.

"I don't want you upsetting her. She might take off again! She needs to know we're on her side."

"She's a married woman now. She won't take off, and she probably doesn't need you quite as much as you think she does."

That stung. "Yes, she does. We were the only stable part of

her life after her parents and Jack died. We were all she had left."

"Yes, but that was a long time ago," Michael said, "and now she has a husband. You can't be her savior, Gayle."

"I'm not! I know I'm not! But she does need me. All of us." Gayle felt sick, shocked into facing her own motives. She didn't really think of herself that way, did she?

"Right now," Michael said, "we just want to talk to her."

TWENTY-ONE

Gayle sipped at the coffee. She'd been trying to acquire a taste for it, just to be sociable and because it was usually the only beverage available in the musicians' lounge, but unless she added milk and sugar, she couldn't get it down.

"If you don't like it, don't drink it." Dot sat opposite her, drinking her own as if it was black nectar. "Bring tea. There must be a place to boil water, isn't there?"

"In the housekeeping room," Gayle said, "but it's awkward to go there, especially since the new head housekeeper quit and they haven't hired another one yet. The women who work there are all about sixteen or over sixty, and they're not friendly. There's a kitchen downstairs, but it's only used for catering special events. We're not supposed to go in there."

"They ought to serve some kind of refreshments during the show," Dot mused. "For the theatergoers, I mean. They could probably make a lot of money that way."

Gayle shuddered. "What a mess that would be. It seems tacky, too."

"But people are already buying food and bringing it in

with them. The theater could make more money if they sold candy and Coke themselves."

"A sticky mess," Gayle said. "We're already having cleaning problems."

"Then something dry, like popcorn or crackers." Dot refilled her cup. "I'd pay money for it, if I had any."

"You need a job," Gayle said. "We're hiring at the theater. You'd make a good housekeeper."

Dot grinned. "Is that sarcasm? I cleaned the bathroom already today, and it's your turn to do the kitchen. I'm off to school in just a few minutes." She glanced at the clock and rose, setting her cup in the sink. "Now, in fact. The streetcar's been late every morning this week, but I can't count on it."

Gayle stretched out her legs and crossed them at the ankle. "I don't have to be at work until ten. It's a good job."

Dot snorted. "At least my school is safe. I mean, no one's being murdered. I'm surprised Papa hasn't talked to you about it."

"About quitting my job?" Gayle asked. "I don't think I'm in any danger. I'm just a bystander, as confused as the police. They seem to be at a standstill. Baffled." She cast an innocent glance at the man who had just entered the kitchen, but Michael didn't respond with his customary remarks.

He looked at Dot. "Off to school, are you?"

She raised her brows. "Yes, I am. Is that a not-so-subtle way of telling me you want to talk to Gayle alone?"

"Subtle or not," he said, "I need to talk to Gayle alone." He waited, stolid and unsmiling, until his youngest sister-in-law hoisted her bag over her shoulder and left.

Gayle stood. "Has something happened?" She thought of the money she'd discovered in her portfolio. The orb. The lamp. "What is it?"

"Hewitt Langdon—his body—was found this morning."

She stared at him for several seconds before dropping back into her chair.

"His body?"

Michael nodded. "And he hasn't been dead long. The doctor said it's been less than two days."

"How do they know these things?" Gayle asked. "No, don't tell me. But two days…do you know what he's been doing all this time?"

Her brother-in-law took the chair Dot had just vacated. "We don't know yet. He had money in his pockets—several fifty-dollar bills, like the ones you turned in to that church in Lake Geneva—and an expensive watch, so he wasn't robbed."

"How did he die?" Gayle hoped he hadn't been hit on the head. It must be related to the theater, of course, but that would be too much, somehow.

"Shot." Michael rose to get a cup of coffee. "That's all we know, so far. We're having to interview everyone again."

"I can't believe he's dead! Is it possible he committed those other murders at the theater and his own death was related to something else?"

He raised his brows. "Unrelated to the other murders?"

"It's already a lot of murder!" Gayle said. "And if he wasn't the murderer, it may not be finished yet."

"True, and two of the victims have been organists."

"Don't say that." Gayle glanced over her shoulder. "Papa hasn't said much about that yet, but I can tell he's worried."

"He should be. If Bridget were in your position, I would request that she leave her job immediately."

"But I'm twenty-five years old, not four." Gayle said in exasperation, "And I like my job."

"You'll like it better if you're alive," Michael said, "and that's the point."

"Where did you find him?"

"Out at Staynes Lake, in an old cabin. There were signs of occupancy, but not what you might expect if he was living there—not exactly." Michael said. "It's part of a camp that's been closed up since before the war. We're tracking down the owner now."

"Is it far from here?"

"An hour's drive and not close to a train. We didn't find an automobile, and it's been too dry to find tire tracks." He finished his coffee and rose. "We'll find out the truth, but I think you ought to consider quitting this job and finding something safer."

"Like playing at a dance hall?" Gayle asked. "That wasn't so safe in New York!"

Michael sat. "What happened in New York? I haven't heard anything about you having problems there."

"No one has." Gayle looked over her shoulder again and lowered her voice, grateful that her father's work required a soundproof door. "I took a job at a dance hall—a legal, perfectly respectable dance hall!—near the college. At least, I thought it was."

"Ah. You always were a naïve child."

The hint of a smile in his voice encouraged her to continue. "One night, as I was naïvely playing on, a group of men with guns pushed through the door and started shouting. I thought they were gangsters at first," she confessed, "and I hid under the piano."

"What happened?" Michael wasn't smiling anymore.

Gayle wished she hadn't said anything, but it was too late to stop. "When I realized they were police—prohis, I crawled out and tried to get to the door. Everyone else was pushing that way, too, but there were more police officers there. Some of the people, including the waiters, were rushing the other direction, and they got out a door on the other wall. I didn't even know it was there!"

Her brother-in-law shook his head. "Did you get arrested?"

"No, but they made me wait there for a while, along with everyone else. In the end, they took away a few of the management people and the rest of the waiters. They started to take some of the girls, too, but a man told them to stop. They had the people they wanted, and the rest of us could leave."

"That was lucky for you," Michael said. "I heard they're trying to arrest the heads of these places now and not so many of the clients. The jails and courts were full of otherwise-respectable people. No real policing is being done at all, even though crime is getting worse." He brooded. "Motorcars make it so much easier for criminals of every sort. Even with four murders and the district attorney hounding us, we can't get enough men because they are all out with Prohis."

She hurried on, committed to the story and hoping to distract Michael from his perpetual complaint. "I didn't tell anyone about it, but in the paper next day, I saw that they really served alcohol there."

Michael rolled his eyes.

"They had a sort of pit in the kitchen, hidden under a big cabinet, and the prohibition agents caught them tossing bottles of liquor into it. There was some kind of code. A customer would order a cup of tea, meaning that they wanted a certain kind of alcohol, or ginger ale, to get another kind. I'd been there for a month, and I had no idea!"

"Naïve. It's here in Chicago, too," he said. "Restaurants and dance halls that really are legitimate businesses, but if you go through a hidden door, you enter another club that isn't so innocent."

"Yes, well, I saw one of those, too, when I was out with some classmates, but I didn't go inside. I'm not stupid, and after that experience, I didn't work anymore except when I could get a gig for a wedding or church service. I didn't even go out much." Gayle grimaced. "I developed a reputation for being a bluenose, and most of the other students avoided me. I was glad when the course was over, and I could come home."

"You should never have gone there," Michael said.

"No, because otherwise I wouldn't have gotten this job here, and I did talk Lillian into returning with me." She touched his arm. "Please don't tell Papa. He'd be upset, even though it's over and I stopped playing there. I know he didn't want me to go out there. He didn't say so, but I think he saw there wasn't anything for me to do here."

"You could have found a job as a teacher or in some other profession," Michael said, "or you could have married."

"I didn't see any men lining up to ask me," Gayle retorted, "and I was too young. I didn't want to get married. Not yet."

He shrugged and stood. "I don't see any reason to tell anyone about it. We have other problems right now, and he may object to those even more than the other."

Her father wouldn't make her quit her job. She was an adult. Gayle didn't want to distress him, though, and it would cause a rift in their good relationship if he asked her to find a new job and she refused.

"There's something else."

Michael sighed. "Of course, there is."

"I think Papa may have met Mr. Glassman before he died. He was talking about the Empire and said he'd met the man who died. He said the newspapers called it an accident."

Michael furrowed his brow. "I'll have to talk to him. Are you going to the theater today?"

She nodded. "I'll be leaving soon. I suppose you and all the other police officers will be there?"

"As many as the Prohis can spare." Michael settled his hat on his head and nodded. "Try to stay out of trouble there. Don't talk to people more than you have to. Besides, I think your boss—Bennet, not Starek—would be glad of an excuse to fire you. You aren't very popular there, are you?"

"It's not my fault," Gayle said. "I don't think Mr. Bennet liked Mr. Langdon very much, and Mr. Langdon hired me without asking him. Or something like that. Men facing off against each other, puffing out their chests."

"Don't make comments like that at the theater," Michael said. "That place is full of gossips. Everyone knew about your quarrels with the other organist, from the orchestra members to the cleaning women. Even the maintenance men talked about it."

Gayle slumped in her chair. "It was all his fault."

"And now he's dead, so don't go saying that, either. Like I said, just don't talk much." Michael left, closing the kitchen door behind him.

TWENTY-TWO

John stared at the man opposite him. Two other police officers prowled the office, but Detective Ashe sat in the red velvet guest chair, calmly requesting a room in which he might interview the Empire employees. All of them.

"Of course. There are three reception rooms on the third level. You can have any of them. All of them. This is horrible." John rubbed his eyes. "Why is this happening?"

"We can't say yet," the detective said, "but we have something to work with now."

"Something to work with?"

"We have a body found somewhere else," Ashe said, "and we'll find the owner of that property. There were signs that someone had lived there recently. A squatter, probably. It didn't look like a place Langdon would stay, since he had plenty of money in his pockets, but if he were hiding, you never know." He drummed his fingers on John's desk. "He'd have to get food, and someone will have seen him, in such a rural location. In the city, no one would notice a stranger, but out there, people will remember him."

"He wasn't in the city, then?" John asked. "Where was he?"

The detective regarded him for a few seconds. "Where were you on Thursday night?"

"Here," John said. "I stayed for the evening show. So many of the staff have left, and Miss Fisher hasn't been able to replace them. Thursday night? You mean that's when he was killed? How did he die?"

"Miss Fisher is the woman who took over the position of theater manager. Is that right?" The detective pulled out his notebook.

"Yes, she was his assistant. She's been the assistant manager since I began here, in fact, before Langdon arrived." And she was getting to be as nervous as the rest of the employees. John hoped she wouldn't quit, too. That would signal the end of the Empire—literally.

"We'll want to interview her first."

"I'll telephone her," John said. When he'd finished, he sat back with a frown. "I have to admit…I thought Langdon must be the murderer."

"As did we," the policeman said, "and maybe he was involved. Miss Nagle seemed quite certain that it was Langdon who pushed her into the street."

"He killed Glassman, Ernie and Jesse Erwin? And then someone else killed him?" It seemed unlikely to John, but then, all of it seemed unlikely. "And I meant to ask you…do you think our organist—both of them—might be in danger? Two of the victims were organists."

"Miss Wells is fairly new here. Do you have reason to believe she knew Langdon before starting this job?"

"I don't think so. Her father is a minister at the Presbyterian church."

His endorsement didn't seem to impress the detective. "What do you know about her?"

"She's a talented organist. I don't believe she knew anyone

here before she started the job. Why? You can't possibly suspect her."

"We are looking at all possibilities," Ashe said imperturbably. "And were you acquainted with Miss Wells previous to her employment here?"

John shook his head. "No, I wasn't. We'd never met."

"And yet, she traveled to Lake Geneva with you."

"No!" John jerked forward. "That's not how it was. My grandparents hired her to perform at their wedding. Their anniversary party, in Lake Geneva. She didn't travel with me at all, and she stayed with friends there—the Fanshaws."

"So, you don't have a personal relationship with her?" Detective Ashe asked.

"No! I…I like her, but we have no connection outside the theater."

"Except for the weekend in Lake Geneva." The detective turned over a page in his notebook. "The entire staff of the Empire seems to think you have a special interest in Miss Wells."

John squirmed. There was no good answer to that. Calling it a special interest sounded…dirty. But he couldn't deny he was attracted to her, either.

Ashe pulled out a pencil and held it, waiting, over the page. John scowled, and after a few seconds, the detective asked, "Have you ever visited the Staynes Lake Camp, Mr. Starek?"

"I don't think so," John said. "Is that where Langdon's body was found?"

A movement at the door caught John's attention. The theater manager stood there, pale and swaying. She grasped the door frame for support. John hastened around his desk and pulled a chair to her.

"Sit down. Are you all right?"

She stared at him and then at the detective. "Mr. Langdon is dead?"

"Shot in the head," the detective said. "Do you know anything about it?"

John frowned at the man's offensive attitude. Miss Fisher was shocked by the news, especially in the current circumstances. He hoped she didn't quit.

She shook her head, curls bobbing wildly. "I don't understand. I thought…but…" She buried her face in her hands.

"What did you think, Miss Fisher?" Ashe asked.

John was torn between reminding him there was a private room for interrogations and the desire to protect the woman. "We all thought Langdon was the killer," he said. "It seemed obvious."

Detective Ashe turned to him. "Why did you think that?"

"He disappeared," John said, "and who else could it have been?"

"Any of a number of people," said Ashe. "Can you show us to one of those reception rooms, please? Miss Fisher, I'd like you to accompany us. Because you worked for Mr. Langdon, you knew him better than most people here. We need more information about the day he disappeared."

She started to stand, dropped down and then used the back of the chair to push herself to her feet. "Yes. I told you before…I don't know anything. He didn't keep a regular schedule."

Ashe turned to John. "Thank you for your time. My men will be searching the theater and talking to people as well."

John wondered if he should ask for a search warrant. Or had he given them permission last time they spoke? He nodded. They had to find what they were looking for—a killer, loose in the Empire.

TWENTY-THREE

Gayle opened her napkin in her lap and relaxed in the warmth of the dining room. Her mother beamed around the table as she set the second roast chicken in front of her husband. "It's been so long since we had everyone together!"

It had been a while. Her father looked pleased, too, surveying his family with satisfaction. Michael and Ruth, with their children spaced between them, looked nervous. Little Maggie was already pulling her silverware off the table and reaching for the saltcellar. Last time, she'd poured her soup into Ruth's lap. Not a simple spill…she'd poured.

"It's a great blessing not afforded to many men," her father said. "A quiverful of arrows and olive sprouts."

"You're an olive sprout," Bridget said to her little sister. Maggie tried to smack her, but Michael intervened.

"If we could only have Lillian here, that would be even better," Gayle said.

"Lillian has a family of her own now," her mother said. "As much as we love her, it's good for her to spend Sundays with her own family."

"Just Willie," Dot said. "And he probably doesn't care about Sunday dinner."

"And William's mother. She might care. She's been a widow for a long time, and he's an only child. Now she has a daughter, and I'm sure she's looking forward to grandchildren, too." Their mother cast a doting smile at Maggie, who dropped her fork on the floor. Diving to retrieve it, she knocked her head on the table and howled. Both parents pushed their chairs back to investigate, Ruth with anxiety, Michael with resignation.

Papa sliced into the chicken and laid the first slice on his wife's plate. "There you go, dear. Ruth, do you want dark meat?" He continued his routine, serving the women first, according to their ages, then Michael, and then himself before serving the children. Ruth had asked once if she could put a plate together for the children before the rest of them, and he had reproached her. "There is an order to these things, Ruth. It's good for them to learn."

Gayle couldn't restrain herself any longer. "Papa, did you say you'd met that other organist from the Empire? Henry Glassman?"

He paused, holding the ladle of gravy over his potatoes. "Yes, briefly. It's not a topic for the dinner table."

"Oh, sorry." Gayle glanced at Michael.

"Perhaps we could talk about it after dinner, sir? Privately?" His voice held just a faint note of the official.

"We can, but I'm not sure how much I can share. What he said was in the nature of a confession, and while I do not condone the practice of that sacrament in our church, he said it to me as a minister, in confidence."

"A confession?" Michael seized on the words and then wiped gravy off his arm, scowling at his daughter. She kissed the arm, and he rolled his eyes before ruffling her hair. "After dinner, then."

The children kept the meal interesting. Sunday dinner had

been so dull before they arrived. Would she ever have children of her own? Gayle wrinkled her nose as Bridget spat her chicken into her hand. Ruth wiped it out with a napkin and a scold. As far as Gayle could tell, just teaching them manners was a full-time job. Ruth tried. Even Michael tried. Bridget was a lively and willful child.

"You know," her mother said, "Bridget reminds me so much of you, Gayle."

Michael snickered. "When she was a child, or now?"

Their mother ignored him. "You had that bright, curious streak, too. You wanted to try everything, touch everything… but you were always easily distracted and then behaved again."

"As far as I can tell," Ruth said, "she hasn't changed much."

Gayle thought about throwing a roll at her sister but decided it would set a bad example for the children. On the other hand, it would serve Ruth right if her children took up roll-throwing.

"The man thought you were a Catholic priest?" Ruth asked. "They take confession and forgive sins, right? He wanted to confess something to you?"

"I think he was confused," their father said. "He wanted to do the right thing. He said he'd got religion." He sighed. "I don't know where he'd got it from. He was trying to follow a lot of rules."

"Well," their mother said, "there are rules, but that's not one of them. Did you set him straight?"

"I was on my way to a missionary support meeting, and I asked him to come back later in the afternoon. He never showed up. I read about his death in the paper the next day." He glanced at the children, who were, for once, sitting upright and listening to him with wide eyes. "He went to live with Jesus in Heaven."

"After all," Dot said, "he had got religion." At her father's frown of disapproval, she started cutting up her chicken, gaze focused on her plate. "Sorry."

"We can talk about it after dinner," Michael said. He removed the glass of milk from his daughter's hand before she could pour it on the linoleum rug. "No, Maggie lass, we aren't doing that again."

"I wish they made glasses better suited to children," Ruth said. "I should bring a couple of our tin ones over here. They still spill them, but at least the tin cups don't shatter."

"She's not spilling," Michael muttered. At a pointed look from his wife, he returned to his own dinner.

"We have some news," Ruth said.

Delicate language for having another baby. Gayle smiled. "Congratulations."

"Oh!" Their mother jumped up and hurried around the table to hug her favorite daughter. "That's wonderful news."

"I didn't even say what the news is," Ruth objected.

"Oh, a mother knows." Her mother patted her cheek. "You're glowing."

"Maybe it will be a boy this time," Dot said.

"I hope so," Michael said. "Your father and I could use a little support here."

"A boy would be so nice." Their mother returned to her seat. "You can raise him up to respect women and care about the poor and underprivileged. To be an advocate for change."

"Of course," Michael said. He used his napkin to hide a smile. "We wouldn't have it any other way."

"We need good men in political office," she continued. "Women, too. If only the Prohibition party had won the election, we would have Marie Brehm as vice-president of the United States right now. Still, she does good work as president of the national party. Do you want more peas, dear?"

Gayle grinned. She enjoyed her mother's mixed personality—militant feminist, suffragette, and prohibitionist—and devoted homemaker who treated her husband like a king. In return, her husband encouraged her in all her endeavors, patiently listening to periodic lectures, and on two occasions, bailing her out of jail. It was a remarkable marriage, and in some ways, it was just what Gayle wanted for herself, eventually.

The meal became tedious by the time their mother brought in the pineapple upside down cake, everyone's patience worn thin at the growing restlessness of the children. Had she really been that mischievous? Gayle didn't remember it that way at all.

Gayle paced the hallway, fuming. She was the one who'd put the pieces together, remembering her father's comments the day of her first performance and later, when they'd talked about her trip to Lake Geneva. She'd been the one to tell Michael about it. Gayle was the organist, so she was directly involved. It was outrageous to exclude her from their discussion. Unfair.

She probably could have talked Michael into letting her participate. She might have contributed insights. Her father was made of sterner stuff, though, calmly closing the door in her face. Papa never argued; he just did what he thought was best.

If Gayle got too involved and he started thinking about the pattern of killings, Papa might decide it was too dangerous for his daughter to be at the Empire at all. She kicked at the baseboard. Michael might tell her about it later if she approached it right.

"Is he still in there?" Ruth asked from the living room doorway. "The girls are ready to leave." She looked tired. "I'm ready to leave."

"I'm sure you are. Are you having morning sickness this time?"

"It's awful," Ruth said, "and not just in the mornings. Michael's mother has been taking the girls over to her house most days, and all I do is be sick and sleep. I'm supposed to be using that time to take care of the house and cook, but Michael comes home to sandwiches or pork and beans most days."

"He doesn't mind, does he?"

Ruth shook her head. "No, his mother did a good job of teaching him to help. When you're the oldest of ten children, you learn to cook and clean and help out whether you're a boy or a girl."

JOHN WATCHED Bennet at the organ. The man did a good job, but he didn't have time to do his own job and play the organ as well. He needed to hire someone—probably two people—soon.

Miss Fisher had refused to do it. "That is the responsibility of the music director," she said. "He was very put out when Mr. Langdon hired Miss Wells."

"I just thought maybe it would help to find a few candidates, since he's so busy now," John said meekly.

"I will ask him if wants assistance." Miss Fisher smoothed the calendar on her desk. Every square had neat notations.

"You still haven't found an assistant for yourself, have you?" he asked.

"I did," she said, "but he didn't work out."

She'd hired a male assistant. John coughed to hide his chuckle. "I'm sorry. I know things are a mess here right now, so let me know if there's any way I can help."

"Things are not a mess here," she said. "Everything is going quite smoothly."

Except for a string of murders. John regarded her. She looked exhausted, and her blouse was rumpled, as if she'd slept in it. "You should make a priority of finding a new assistant," he said. "I'd like you to do that today, if possible."

"Every show has been on schedule. Ticket sales are up."

"There's no such thing as bad publicity," John said. "I can't be glad that sales are up, when it's because of the scandal and excitement."

"But I've managed all of it." She laid her hands flat on the desk.

John noticed that her nails were bitten short, her cuticles broken and red. "I think we should consider shutting down the theater for a while."

"No!" She sprang to her feet, knocking her chair over. "Everything is under control! I got a new head housekeeper and replaced everyone else who quit. We're on schedule. Besides, all the vaudeville troupes and other shows are lined up, and we'd have to pay them whether they perform or not."

"That doesn't matter. We can close until the police arrest the killer and then reopen." He held up a hand. "Or you find yourself an assistant today and stop trying to do everything yourself. Mr. Langdon didn't try to do it all himself."

"He didn't do any of it."

John wasn't sure he'd heard her correctly, and he didn't want to go down that rabbit trail. "Find an assistant," he repeated, "and start delegating some of the work. I don't want to see you here from dawn to midnight like Langdon was."

"I don't need to be here that much to keep everything running smoothly."

The stiff response worried him. Being an employer was more complicated than he had expected. He hadn't meant to offend her. He hadn't realized how sensitive she was before, to implications that she couldn't do her job. She'd always seemed so…competent. A string of murders was enough to unsettle most people, but he hadn't expected Miss Fisher to unravel.

TWENTY-FOUR

John stopped at the sight of Michael Brady leaving the manager's office.

"Sergeant Brady. Is everything all right?" He winced at the stupid question.

"No, it is not all right. I am looking for the manager, and her new assistant tells me she is gone."

"Gone?" Sickness roiled in John's stomach. "Missing?"

"No," Brady said. "She went home early. Her assistant says she looked sick, but Miss Fisher told her she might be back later. She gave the woman no instructions but left a message for her to give her brother if he happened to call."

"A message for Miss Fisher's brother?"

Brady nodded. "That's all she told the assistant. And that she might be back."

"Do you know what the message is?" John asked.

"He is to clean up and then stay home. Be careful." Brady quoted the message. "That's all. Do you know much about this Miss Fisher, sir?"

"She's been here longer than I have," John said. "She was the assistant to the manager who left when my grandfather took over."

"Why did he leave?"

John shrugged uncomfortably. "Some of them did. The Imperial Brotherhood fellows didn't mind taking his money, and the staff didn't care who was paying their wages as long as he wasn't actively involved, but when he bought them out and handed over the business to me, some of the staff didn't like it. Grandfather is a Christian now, but he's still a Jew. I don't say that's why all of them left, but maybe the manager was one of them. I don't think any of the current staff have a problem with it." John was two generations removed, though, with a different last name.

"Ah." Brady nodded. "The world is like that, sometimes. So, some of the staff left. Can you tell me who they were?" He took out his notebook and pencil.

"I don't know all the names, but I can tell you which positions I had to fill." He nodded toward the stairs. "Let's go up to my office, and I'll tell you what I know. Miss Fisher has all the details, of course. I don't think we lost many of the general employees during the changeover. It was the management and senior staff, mostly."

"Was there anyone who seemed angry when he left?" Brady asked.

"Not that I know of," John said. "I was busy replacing them, with my grandfather's help. He helped me get set up and then left it to me. I thought things were going well." He sounded like Miss Fisher.

"Did you have to fire anyone when you took over?"

John shook his head. "I don't think so. I can ask Miss Fisher to check on that and get you the other names. There was the theater manager, the chief accountant, the head of the stagehands, the music director…" He ticked them off on his fingers. "The chief projectionist, and a creative director, too, but I'm not quite sure what he did. Langdon didn't replace him, and I don't think it's made a difference."

"You don't remember any of their names?" Brady asked.

"They were all gone by the time I arrived," John said apologetically, "and I was busy replacing them. Oh, I think the accountant's name was Brown. We checked to make sure he hadn't been embezzling, but there wasn't anything there. Have a seat."

Brady sat. "What about the organist?"

"Erwin had been here a long time," John said. "As soon as they started showing films, I think. He made a point of coming to see me right away, to make sure I knew he was the union representative."

"What about Mr. Glassman?" Brady asked.

"I don't know much about him. He seemed to be a good organist, and not as rude as Erwin. Quiet." John turned up his hands in a shrug. "I don't know why anyone would want to kill him, but then, I don't know why any of them were killed. There must be a connection, but I don't see it."

"Could he have been killed to create an opening for another organist?"

"You mean for Miss Wells? Your sister?" John asked incredulously. "I don't know why they would. Besides, I'm afraid she's had a rough time here. The men haven't been helpful or friendly."

"Mr. Langdon hired her," Brady said, "and it wasn't usually his responsibility. People here seem to feel strongly about their job positions and responsibilities."

"Yes, but…there was still an opening. We need three organists to work all the shows. Erwin and Glassman were covering them, but we needed to hire another, even before Glassman was killed. Bennet can fill in when he has to, but it's not ideal."

Brady made a note. "And you got another organist after you hired Gayle—Miss Wells."

"Yes, but I really didn't have anything to do with that. I know she was upset about it," John said. "Erwin was rotten to her, and Bennet wasn't much better."

"That organist—Shores—did he know anyone here before he was hired?" Brady asked. "Who hired him?"

"That would have been Bennet. Shores worked at the Roxy on Bridge Street, and when it burned down, he came here. We took on a couple of their other people, too."

The police officer rubbed his neck. "I'm losing track of your organists. At some point, you had three. Did one leave before Glassman was killed?"

"I don't know. Maybe they left when Grandfather took over," John said. "I hope Miss Fisher returns soon. I'm afraid I'm not being very helpful."

"You don't know anything about Henry Glassman?"

"I know he didn't have any family. Miss Fisher talked to his landlady. His rent was paid up, and there wasn't much else we could do for him. We paid his burial expenses, but…" John shook his head. "I was out of town when he died, and I didn't find out until I returned and met your sister. She told me about it."

"Gayle told you that Glassman was dead?" Brady asked. "How did that conversation happen?"

John didn't know if Brady was asking as a police officer or a big brother. "I met her in the lobby. She was trying to find Langdon, to finalize her employment here. She told me she was the new organist, and I asked about Glassman."

"I see." Michael tapped his pencil on the marble desk. "I will talk to Miss Fisher when she returns, but I'd like to know more about Henry Glassman. Did he have any particular friends here?"

"I don't know," John said again. "He would have worked most closely with Jesse Erwin and Bennet. The organist practices with the orchestra sometimes, so he may have known some of the other musicians. I didn't know him well enough to say, though."

Brady considered him, silent long enough to make John fidget, tempted to babble. Finally, the police officer leaned back in the chair. "In your opinion, was Henry Glassman a religious man?"

"Religious?" Surprised, John folded his hands on his desk and sat forward. "I don't know. I never had a conversation with him. What would that have to do with his death?"

"Before he died, Glassman tried to make confession. A priest would hear his sins and issue forgiveness, in confidence. Unfortunately for Mr. Glassman, he didn't realize that's only a Catholic practice. He approached a protestant minister by mistake."

John wondered if Michael Brady was Catholic. Most Irishmen were, weren't they?

"The minister, from a church not far from here…"

His father-in-law, no doubt, from the way he avoided details. John waited.

"Mr. Glassman said he had been guilty of many sins and had come to Chicago with the intention of continuing on the same wicked path. He'd been delivered, he said, and was going straight. He said something about not being able to persuade his friends. At first, the minister thought the man had been to a temperance meeting or Billy Sunday revival, but then Glassman said he didn't know what to do. He didn't want to go to jail or be a snitch." John consulted his notes. "The minister wanted to explain to him about not needing to go to confession, but he was in a hurry and asked the man to come back later. He never showed up, and the minister saw the death notice in the paper a few days later."

"He didn't contact the police?" John asked.

"It didn't seem necessary at the time. It was reported as an accident," Brady said, "and the man hadn't seemed frightened or suicidal. And even though the man was a stranger, he had approached…this minister as a confessor. He felt it was confidential. It was only later, after Erwin's death, that he decided to talk to me."

"Ah. So maybe his friends thought he might snitch on

them." John rubbed his jaw. "That's interesting. It sounds like a real clue."

Brady closed his notepad and slid it into his pocket. "We are looking for confirmation that Glassman had some kind of criminal or immoral past and had changed. Did you see anything of that kind?"

"No," John said. "I didn't know him well enough, and I don't know who his friends would have been. Talk to Bennet. He can probably tell you."

Michael stood and nodded. "Thank you. I will be doing that. I would be grateful if you would send someone to find me when Miss Fisher returns, also."

John watched him leave, wondering if there had been more to the reported confession than Brady had shared. What would a middle-aged theater organist consider to be a wicked path? Drinking or gambling, he supposed. They were the most common vices, and even ordinary people indulged in them. Few of those people actually went to jail for them—at least, not for long. The Prohibition agents were more interested in those who manufactured and sold the liquor. The owners of the illegal clubs and casinos. Why would an organist be in danger?

HADN'T they just played this scene? The detective sitting opposite John seemed more relaxed and confident today. Cocky, almost.

"I came to inform you, as a courtesy, that we have arrested Eugenia Fisher, and she will be formally charged tomorrow for the murder of Hewitt Langdon."

"Miss Fisher?" John dropped his pen. "She killed Langdon?"

"We believe that she and her brother, James Fisher, colluded to kidnap and murder Langdon so she could take over his job," Ashe said. "We are investigating the possibility that Miss Ernst was involved as well."

"Ernie?"

"It's hard to say at this point," Ashe said. "She may have become frightened after the actual kidnapping and threatened to tell the police. Erwin could have witnessed it or found out later, too."

It didn't make sense. "But what about Glassman?"

Ashe shrugged. "An accident, just as we thought."

"Are you sure?"

"We have evidence and a confession," the detective said. "Two confessions, both of them trying to protect the other, but we'll get to the truth."

"Miss Fisher's brother?" The one who was supposed to clean up and stay home, according to Sergeant Brady.

"We believe he was the one who actually kidnapped Langdon," Ashe said. "He lured him out of the theater by telling him his motorcar had been vandalized. Outside, he hit Langdon over the head—not a killing blow—and then chloroformed him."

"But what good would a kidnapping do?" John asked. "If they weren't going to kill him, they'd have to let him go eventually, and then he'd go straight to the police and have them arrested."

"Well, the boy is seventeen," the detective said, "and none too bright. He was apprenticed to a druggist for a while, but they demoted him to delivery boy when he couldn't keep up with the real work. He got his hands on chloroform, though, and knew how to use it." He smirked. "Probably from watching your movies. Once he had Langdon unconscious, he put him in the druggist's van and drove him up to an old cabin at Staynes Lake. It turns out that property used to be owned by some people named Fisher. A great-uncle or some such relation of these two. We figured that one out right away. There was evidence of ropes, too. The boy had tied him up."

"But you can't think Miss Fisher was involved. I mean… Miss Fisher is so…competent." John stopped, conscious of the ridiculous argument.

"The boy says she didn't know until later. She says it was all her plan, and he's innocent." Ashe shrugged. "We'll get the truth out of them. What can you tell me about her?"

"Miss Fisher? She's been there longer than anyone."

"As the assistant manager," Ashe said. "It sounds like she was tired of being an assistant. Did you have any reason to believe she was dissatisfied in her position at the Empire?"

"No. At least, I don't think so." She'd made that comment about Langdon not working, but she'd never complained.

"Did she apply for the theater manager position when the former one left, before you hired Langdon?"

"I don't think so." John closed his eyes to concentrate. "There were a few applicants, but none so well-qualified as Langdon. I think I would have remembered if she had asked for the job."

"If she had asked for it," the detective asked, "would you have given it to her?"

"I don't know. Probably. I'd never done any real hiring before. I wouldn't have a problem hiring a woman for the job, if that's what you mean."

"Did she ask for the job after Langdon disappeared?"

They were back to the interrogation format. John shook his head, glad to have a question with a positive answer. "No, not at all. When I offered her the job, she seemed reluctant. She wanted to know what would happen if Langdon came back."

Ashe made a note. "And what did you tell her?"

"I said he'd lost my trust and I wouldn't take him back. The job was hers, permanently."

"And she was happy with the promotion? Has she done a good job at it?"

"Yes. I think she was probably doing the job all along,"

John said frankly. "Assistants do get stuck with most of the work, and she's very competent."

"Which might make her resentful. Did she seem to think Mr. Langdon would return?"

"I don't know," John said. "She said something about…" John tried to remember her words. "She wanted to know if he would get the job back if it wasn't his fault. If he'd been prevented from coming back, somehow."

"Interesting." Ashe wrote in his book. "If it wasn't his fault."

TWENTY-FIVE

If he had any dark secrets, John would have spilled them. Not even his college pranks had landed him in a police station before, and he was taken aback by the guilt-inducing atmosphere. Detective Ashe said he needed him there, rather than at the theater, because he had something to show him. John had a hunch it might be a matter of wanting control of the interview. At the theater, Ashe had to sit in the visitor chair.

"There you are." The detective held open his office door. "Come in. Sit down."

The cluttered office was bleak, with a row of windows overlooking a sooty brick wall. Ashe returned to his seat behind the utilitarian desk, and John set his hat on one of the two wooden chairs before sitting in the other.

"Good morning."

"Good morning." Ashe picked up a file and dropped it back on the desk. "We finally got an identification on the man calling himself Hewitt Langdon."

It took John a few seconds to process the blunt statement. "Calling himself? You mean that wasn't his name?"

"Only recently. Until he moved to Chicago, he was known

as George Siegel. He ran a series of clubs in New York. Was arrested a few times, but they could never hold him. That probably wasn't his real name, either, and we'll keep working on it."

"But he had great theater references!" John said. "Written references, and I telephoned two of them and they raved about him."

"Do you still have his past employment history? The names of the theaters and people he claimed to have worked for?" Ashe pulled a notebook toward himself and took a pen from his drawer.

John rubbed the back of his neck. "One was the Odeon on Broadway. I went there once when I visited New York a few years ago. It burned down shortly after that. I think he was at the Regent then, and I know I telephoned them. They must have called him Langdon, too, or I wouldn't have known who they meant."

"I'd appreciate it if you'd get me those names and numbers. Whatever you have."

"Of course. I'll have it sent over here," John said. "He seemed to know the job, so he must have managed a theater before, somewhere, whatever his name was. Are you sure it's the same man?"

Ashe shoved a photo across the table. It was a classic mug shot, with a bored Langdon staring into the camera, head slightly tilted. "He was also mixed up with the Dutch Schultz gang. Not leadership, but hanging around the edges."

"The mob? Are you sure?" John shook his head to clear it. "Sorry. It's just so incredible."

Ashe raised his brows. "More incredible than having four unrelated murders at the Empire?"

"I knew they had to be related," John said, "but the mob just seems too much. You arrested Miss Fisher and her brother. Do you still think they killed him?"

"They haven't been formally charged," the detective said.

"It's possible that Eugenia Fisher worked with Dutch Schultz or some of the other New York boys to get Siegel out of the way."

John frowned. "You can't honestly believe that Miss Fisher is in cahoots with the mob. If they wanted Siegel and knew he was at the theater, they'd just go in and get him themselves—not hire a kid or a woman to kidnap him."

"So maybe they acted independently and kidnapped him so she could have his job, just like we said yesterday," Ashe said. "Maybe it really was a coincidence. He could have killed Glassman before he was kidnapped. We just received this new information, so we're still investigating."

"That seems like a lot of coincidence," John said. "Did Ernie participate in the kidnapping and then get cold feet, or did Langdon—Siegel—kill her because she learned he was stealing or had a false name or a criminal record?"

"Siegel, most likely. He was up to something. Glassman…" Ashe tapped his pen on the desk, appearing to hesitate. "Glassman's death opened up a job at the Empire. The organist job. And Langdon—Siegel—hired Miss Wells, who had also just arrived from New York."

"Oh, that's ridiculous," John said. "She's from Chicago. Her family's here."

"If—I'm just saying if—she was involved, her local connections would be useful to Siegel."

John fought the impulse to jump to his feet and yell at the man. "Her connections are in the Presbyterian church. Her father's a minister, and her mother's a member of the Temperance Union and does all kinds of charitable works!"

Ashe shrugged. "Speculation. But the timing is right, and her hiring was suspicious. Why did Siegel hire her at all? Normally, that would have been the responsibility of the music director."

That had been strange, but Gayle was innocent. John knew it beyond the shadow of a doubt. He rocked in his chair, searching for words that would show the detective it was all a crazy coincidence.

"There's money involved, too," Ashe went on. "Siegel had cash sitting out on a desk in his apartment and on his body when he was found. Fifty-dollar bills. The New York police say it might be from gambling—numbers and casinos inside a club run by Siegel. There's a rumor he took off with it, leaving town without paying the mob their cut."

"Wouldn't they just follow him here?" John asked.

"Not if he handled it right. Even if they knew he came to Chicago, the mob there can't ask Torrio or Capone for help locating their own man. They'd lose face."

The infamous names made it real and yet unreal. It made John feel sick to think of those names in connection with the Empire. "So, they must have found him," he said, "and killed him. Unless the Fishers did."

"We'll find the truth." Ashe underlined something in his notebook. "We're keeping an eye on everyone at the Empire, because that's where the murders connect, but it's likely that only the first two murders were Siegel's." He ticked them off on his fingers. "Glassman, to open a position, and Ernie, because she found something out. We're still working on Erwin. I wouldn't be surprised if he recognized Siegel from New York. Siegel knew a lot of people out there, in the casinos and speakeasies. A theater isn't much of a place to lay low." He scratched his ear. "I'm surprised he took the risk."

"I don't think he had much of a social life," John said. "He was always at the theater, but he didn't mix with the guests much, as far as I know. And he wouldn't have had to kill Glassman. We need three organists, and there were only two at the time. Miss Wells isn't involved, anyhow."

"She doesn't have a criminal record," Ashe said, "and the police there know nothing about her. They checked her history at our request, and she did go to school there."

"Of course, she did! She has good credentials. I'm sure Langdon wouldn't have hired…" he trailed off.

Ashe waited politely for a few seconds, but when John didn't continue, he leaned back in his chair. "There's a lot of evidence against her. Bad timing. She's lucky she has an alibi for two of the murders."

"She didn't have anything to do with any of it," John said, "and she was a good hire. She's a fine musician, and she's become very popular with the audience."

"Yes, indeed." Ashe consulted his notes. "There was some animosity between her and Jesse Erwin. Everyone in the theater seemed to know about it."

John couldn't deny that. He sought a new topic. "Why come to the Empire at all? I mean, was he really a theater manager at some point?"

"We're working on that. Siegel kept a low profile outside the theater. No friends. His apartment at the Halstead was plush, but it wasn't… personal. The staff at the hotel said he ate at the restaurant frequently, and he was always pleasant but quiet. Tipped well but not extravagantly."

"The fact that he lived at the Halstead House was extravagant," John said. "He was paid well but not enough to live there."

"He was probably living on the money he stole from the mob."

John swallowed. If that was the case, he was grateful the man hadn't been gunned down in the theater lobby.

Ashe pushed the photograph across the table again. "Can you formally identify this as the man you knew as Hewitt Langdon?"

"Yes."

"Had you ever met this man in New York or anywhere else before the day you hired him?"

"No. I told you I hadn't." John watched Ashe make notes.

"Did you pursue your customary hiring practices when he applied for the position of theater manager?"

"I...I didn't have a lot of customary practices then. I'd just taken over the ownership of the theater," John said. His collar was hot. The room was hot. "I checked his references. Some of them."

"And you will send me all of his employment records when you return to the theater?" Ashe appeared to reconsider. "Can you please telephone the theater now and get those sent over here? All of them—Miss Ernst, Erwin, Glassman. And send over Miss Wells', too." He smiled blandly. "Just to be thorough."

"You looked at all of those already," John said.

"Yes, but we'd like to look at them again, here at my office, in light of the new information." Ashe picked up the telephone and talked to the operator. A few seconds later, he handed the telephone to John and waited while John was connected to his secretary.

Aware of the man's eyes on him, John conveyed the request. When he'd finished, Ashe took the phone back without comment. John caught himself running a finger around his collar. Just being in this situation made him feel guilty. The problem, as far as John could see it, was that there were too many suspects. Too many motives. Everyone Ashe mentioned seemed to make sense—except Gayle, of course, and if he didn't know her, he would probably be suspicious of her, too.

"Which departments would Langdon do the hiring for?"

"Most of them," John said. "The music department was different because it was...music. Langdon wouldn't know if a musician was good enough or not, I suppose. So, Bennet does all of that. Langdon probably consulted with the technical people for jobs down there, because they need to make sure they have the skills necessary for the electrical systems or whatever they're doing."

"Housekeeping, stagehands, catering, maintenance, ticket takers, and ushers?"

"Those would all be hired by the theater manager or his assistant," John said, "but from what I've seen, people are recommended. Herb Wilkes, the chief projectionist, brought his brother in and helped him get a job in the maintenance department when he heard there was an opening. The technical people know other technical people. They're all unionized, too, so they work it out among themselves."

"Is that true of the music department?" the detective asked.

"Maybe," John said. "Probably. Bennet could tell you more about them."

"Have you been experiencing thefts at the theater?"

John scowled. "You know we have."

"Do you have a list of the stolen items?" Ashe asked. "And did you report the thefts to the police?"

John felt himself growing warm again. "I have a list, and no, I did not report the thefts."

"That seems unusual. Why not? Do you have a suspicion of who is stealing from you? Are you protecting someone?"

The barrage of questions caught John off guard. "Thousands of people go through the Empire every day. The items were too accessible. It was my fault." His grandfather had made that clear. He hadn't given John such a lecture in ten years. "Things are being rearranged to prevent future thefts."

Ashe shook his head. "It seems strange to me that you'd put valuable things within reach of the crowds."

"Yes, well, I'm not doing it anymore."

"I assume these items were insured?"

Not anymore, but John didn't feel it necessary to share that with the detective. "I'm not filing a claim."

Ashe made more notes. John tugged at his collar. Did this man think he was committing insurance fraud? He'd been guilty of stupidity—naïveté, mostly—hoping that people would enjoy the art—but he hadn't done anything else wrong.

"We're waiting for more information from New York," Ashe said. "They're reviewing the cases involving Siegel, but they don't have any more manpower than we do. The prohibition agents aren't making it a priority, either."

The detective's irritation was encouraging. He'd been so calm and methodical that John had felt irrationally guilty. He seemed a little more human now.

"Do you need anything else from me?" John ventured. "I don't know what else I can tell you."

"Oh, I still have questions for you." Ashe nodded at the papers on his desk. "I'd like to know more about how the Empire passed into your possession, for one thing, and everything you can tell me about the Imperial Grand Council of the Venerable Brotherhood of Peers of the Eastern Mystic Temple. It appears that there might be more to that building than you've shown us."

TWENTY-SIX

John slammed his office door. It wasn't very satisfactory; the heavy door swung into place with a muffled thud that failed to express his frustration. He'd shared every bit of information he could think of, including the two incidents with the vaudeville performers. Ashe had seemed particularly interested in those, especially the one involving Gayle.

When John had reiterated his conviction that Gayle was completely innocent, Ashe had delivered an avuncular lecture on the perils of being taken in by a pretty face.

"It's those proper, lady-like ones you have to watch. That Lillian Nagle…you know exactly what you're getting with a dame like that. She tells you what she thinks and doesn't bother hiding anything. But the quiet ones…they have something to hide."

Gayle had never struck John as quiet. On her first day of work, she'd told him off for letting Ernie fall, implying he was responsible for the unsafe working conditions. She'd marched to Miss Fisher's office to complain that the men weren't treating her with respect. She'd gone off alone to New York for organ training and brought her wayward friend home with her. She might be proper and lady-like, but she wasn't exactly meek.

His musings were interrupted by his secretary's knock.

"Good afternoon, sir." She entered his office and handed him a sheet of paper. "I've been making the calls you requested, and I was just getting ready to call the booking agency when I saw this."

He scanned the letter. In the politest terms, it regretted to inform him that Tobler and Jones would no longer be able to supply acts to the Empire. John looked up. "It looks like our reputation has spread. I hope the other agencies don't blacklist us, too." He tossed the letter on the desk. "You don't need to call them. They'll send us a final bill if we owe them anything. I appreciate your help with this. Our new assistant manager is doing all she can, but she's..."

"She didn't have any training or preparation before Miss Fisher left," his secretary said diplomatically. "She's working on the employee issues."

"I hope she doesn't quit, too," John said. "I can't thank you enough for taking over."

She gave him a quick smile and returned to her office, leaving the letter on his desk. He reread it, trying to gauge its tone. Did they mean they would never send acts again, or could they be persuaded to return once the Empire's problems were cleared up?

The date on the letter caught his attention. It had been sent a week ago, before Jesse Erwin or Langdon had died. Why would they cancel their service then, when the only death had been the housekeeper's?

GAYLE PEEKED IN THE HOUSEKEEPERS' lounge as she passed. Policemen were searching and questioning the staff throughout the theater, but she hadn't seen Michael. It didn't matter. At twenty-five years old, she didn't need her big brother-in-law to hold her hand. It would be a comfort to see him, though, as she waited for her turn to be interviewed. Interrogated.

It would be all right. Except for Michael, no one knew about the items she'd found—the money, orb, and the lamp. She hadn't taken any of them. She was innocent of any crime at all, from theft to murder.

When the word had come that the theater was closing— temporarily, of course—Gayle had done her own searching. She cleaned out her locker, grateful to find nothing had been inserted into it, and checked her pockets and portfolio carefully. Still, that detective didn't like her. Jesse hadn't liked her. Mr. Bennet didn't like her. Gayle sighed and sat on the piano bench. She'd never been disliked before coming here.

"Miss Wells." The young police officer seemed uncomfortable. "Detective Ashe is ready for you." He looked like he was going to say more, but after a few seconds, he turned and led her silently up three flights of stairs to one of the reception rooms.

It was an incongruous setting for a police investigation. Several tables and chairs had been set up, and a telephone wire ran across the ornate carpet to where the detective sat at a square table.

Gayle sat and waited for him to finish his conversation with another man, willing her hands and feet to be still, trying to breathe steadily and not look as frightened as she felt.

"Ah. Miss Wells."

Her heart sank. His tone was all wrong. He sounded as if he had finally discovered the criminal and was about to expose her. Gayle swallowed and smiled tightly. "Detective Ashe."

He leaned back in his chair and regarded her. "We've already spoken several times, but you aren't telling me everything."

"I don't know anything else."

"I find that hard to believe," he said. "You're connected to just about everything that's happened here."

She caught her breath. "No, I'm not."

"Hm. We investigated your background, of course, and we found something you failed to mention."

Did he know about the incident at the dance hall? Michael might have had to tell him. She tried to give a nonchalant shrug. "I can't imagine what that would be."

"We discovered that Michael Brady just happens to be your brother-in-law."

"Oh." Gayle folded her hands tightly. "I don't see what that has to do with any of this."

"You may not," Ashe said, "but Sergeant Brady certainly does. He's been relieved of duty and will be reprimanded."

"Relieved of duty?" Anger overcame fear. "He didn't do anything wrong!"

"We don't know that yet. His reports are being reviewed, and we may need to reexamine all information or evidence he produced."

"That's ridiculous." Gayle narrowed her eyes. It was easier to sit here angry than in fear. Michael would be devastated if he lost his job. What would become of Ruth and their family? "He behaved professionally."

"Maybe so, but he had a responsibility to tell me of the connection when he was assigned to this case, and he deliberately failed to do that. Since you are a...person of interest in this investigation, that makes his involvement suspect."

"There is nothing for him to be involved with!"

"How well did you know George Siegel?"

"What?" Disconcerted, Gayle stared at him. "Who?"

He looked at her with exaggerated patience. "Come now, Miss Wells. I'm not buying that innocent act. You would have called him Siegel in New York, before he changed his name to Hewitt Langdon."

She shook her head emphatically. "I'd never met Mr.

Langdon by any name before I came to the Empire, and I only met him here a few times before he disappeared. I didn't know him at all in New York."

He didn't make a note of that, and some of her anxiety returned. She couldn't let Michael get in trouble.

"You have a friend, Lillian Nagle, who came back from New York at the same time you did. Miss Nagle has a police record."

Gayle winced. She wasn't going to correct the man in regard to Lillian's name.

"Miss Nagle was detained after a raid at one of Siegel's establishments in New York. Although she was not formally charged with a crime, they do have a record of her. Three records, actually, for similar violations related to the Volstead Act."

Poor Lillian. Gayle wondered if she had confessed this to Willie. Of course, he might have been right there at her side, dancing and swigging whiskey.

"I don't know anything about those," she said. "I've known Lillian since we were babies. She wouldn't do anything like theft or murdering people."

He made a show of feigning surprise. "I wasn't implying that she would. I was just helping you see that we do have a connection between you and Siegel."

She gaped at him. "That's a connection? My friend went to an establishment he owned in another city?"

"And then you and Miss Nagle followed him back to Chicago."

"We did not." She stopped, aware that her raised voice was drawing attention. "We came back because I had finished my course of instruction at Eastman School of Music and it was time to come home."

"But why did Miss Nagle come with you?"

"She wanted to come home, too. Ask her yourself!"

Ashe nodded several times. "I would like to do that.

Unfortunately, I haven't been able to locate her yet. She and her husband…" he smiled benignly. "We do know about the husband. They seem to have absconded."

"Absconded?" Outraged, Gayle knocked her chair over as she jumped to her feet. "They went on a honeymoon!"

He seemed unperturbed by her reaction. "Maybe so, but no one knows where they are."

Poor Lillian. If the police had been talking to Willie's mother, Lillian would be mortified. Gayle retrieved her chair and set it upright with excessive force. She glowered at the detective.

"I did not have anything to do with any of the crimes here at the Empire. Whatever Lillian may have done in New York, I doubt that she had anything to do with this Siegel."

Too late, she remembered that Lillian did know Siegel. She knew him well enough to accuse him of throwing her in front of a streetcar. Detective Ashe's use of the different names had confused her.

He leaned back in his chair. "That's the thing. Whether she knew him in New York or not, she did know him here. She accused him of trying to kill her. Why would he want to kill her, unless he believed she would expose him?"

And she probably pressured Langdon—Siegel—into giving Gayle a job, too. Gayle set her jaw. "Did you have more questions for me?"

"Oh, yes. Would you like a cup of coffee before we start?"

JOHN KNOCKED on the door frame and stepped inside the assistant manager's office. She sat up with a start, wide eyes magnified behind her round glasses. She'd never last. He nodded and gave her what he hoped was an encouraging smile.

"How are you doing, Miss Larsen? I'm sorry you had to

join us at such a difficult time. Usually, we go on quite smoothly. My secretary says you're doing a good job with the personnel issues."

"Yes, sir." Her voice held an unexpected streak of practicality. "I'm afraid most of them want to quit, even after I offered them the bonus and their regular wages while we're closed. I'm trying to convince them it's like getting a paid holiday, but…" Her voice trailed off and she handed him a sheaf of papers. "The housekeeping staff all came in together and quit. They say the theater's haunted and dangerous."

"Dangerous, maybe," John said, "but it's only five years old. That's not long enough to get haunted."

"They say ghosts go up and down the stairs at night." She shook her head. "They wanted to tell me all about it—the ghost of Mr. Langdon, floating through the hallways. The organist, playing music in the middle of the night. I let them talk, hoping I could change their minds about leaving, but it was no use. They just got more worked up."

"I'm sorry. We'd better advertise for more staff."

"Yes, sir." The woman didn't actually scoff at the idea, but her opinion was clear. "None of the engineers or maintenance men have left, and only a few of the stagehands."

"Did the stagehands see ghosts, too?" John asked, flipping through the paperwork.

"Only one of them, sir, but he said his sister was a housekeeper, so she probably told him all about it." Miss Larsen pushed her glasses further up the bridge of her nose. "The thing is, most of the employees doubt that you'll be re-opening at all."

"Of course, we'll reopen! What about ushers?"

"About half of them, I'm afraid." She handed him another sheet of paper. "This is the current list of who's staying and who's left."

He grimaced. "Most of the musicians, of course. They'd

be the most upset, I suppose—especially those who were playing the night Erwin was killed."

"Mr. Bennet is staying, sir, and most of the orchestra." Miss Larsen leaned across the desk to indicate names on the list. "Those two—Mr. Hadley and Mr. Klee—came in together. They said they'd stay, and they had other gigs to keep them going in the meantime." She dropped her voice to a whisper. "I think they might have been drinking alcohol, sir."

He tossed the papers back on her desk. "Well, tell Bennet to hire whoever he needs. We'll open again as soon as the police investigation is done."

"Yes, sir." She sat. "Is it true that Miss Fisher killed Mr. Langdon?"

"Who told you that?" John demanded. Ashe said they weren't sharing information about the Fishers, since the news of Langdon's real identity had come immediately after their arrest and they needed more time to sort things out.

"People seem to think she did. Mr. Rogg says he's not a bit surprised. He said theater management isn't a job for a woman." She sniffed.

"It's a confusing situation. The police don't know yet."

"I see. Well, I didn't know Miss Fisher long, but she always seemed so nervous. It's hard to believe she could be a cold-blooded killer."

"Oh, Mickey, I'm so, so sorry!" Gayle hurled herself at his broad chest and burst into sobs.

Michael patted her back. "Hush. It's not your fault. It's all mine. I should have spoken up straightaway, but I didn't expect it to get so big. Don't worry. It'll get straightened out." He blew out a breath. "I may have to wait a little longer for that promotion, though."

"I'm sorry." She pulled back and examined his face. "What did Ruth say?"

He reddened slightly. "I didn't tell her anything yet. I want to see where this goes first. She's been sick, and there's no point in worrying her until we know what there is to worry about."

"That Ashe is a horrible man," Gayle said. "He thinks I did everything."

Michael raised his shoulders in a shrug. "Well, lass, I'd suspect you, too, if I didn't know you."

"Michael!"

"If Ashe knew about the money and the other things, he'd have you locked up by now. Are you sure no one else knows about those?"

"No. John Starek saw the one fifty-dollar bill, but he's never mentioned it again."

Michael scratched his jaw. "He's got a lot of money, so it probably didn't mean much to him. Hopefully, he won't mention it to Ashe."

JOHN ROSE, alarmed by the loud voices in his secretary's office. Before he could get to the connecting door, it burst open, and Ashe strode in. His secretary followed, protesting, until John waved her off. "Thanks, Mrs. Barrow. It's fine." He regarded the detective, who had already dropped into the guest chair as if he owned it. "You only had to ask to see me. No need to push your way in."

"She would have just given me a runaround like everyone else here. My officers are having trouble getting interviews with your staff. Half of them have taken off, even after we told them to stay. Is there an ashtray in here?"

"No. Half of the staff have quit. They just walked out." John sat. "Nothing I could do to stop them."

Ashe put his cigarette case away. "Then I'll need a list of their home addresses." He made no move to rise. "We've been getting some information from New York. Nothing much. It sounds like Siegel just hovered on the edges of the big time. Ambitious but not focused is the way the report reads. He did a little of everything, but his only real success was the club he ran before he came out here. That went big."

"You said he ran from the mob because he had a casino and took off with the money," John said.

"Inside the club. You might call it a speakeasy. It was in the basement of a school, if you can believe it. Those little kiddies never knew what went on in the basement when they were tucked into bed at night." Ashe chuckled. "Lillian Nagle was arrested there once. Your Miss Wells still claims she knows nothing about it."

"Then she probably doesn't," John said. "I have always found her quite truthful."

"Not so truthful," Ashe said. "I told you she kept secrets. Her brother-in-law, Michael Brady, was on the case here, and neither of them mentioned their relationship to me. Needless to say, he's been suspended, and she's still on my suspect list."

Brady had been suspended. John pressed his lips together, refusing to comment. Detective Ashe clearly enjoyed baiting him. After a few seconds, he asked, "How are the Fishers? Do they need legal counsel?"

"They've got it. That Fisher woman insisted on having a public defender, and now they've both clammed up. The boy's a halfwit. First, he said he kidnapped Langdon, then he said he thought the man escaped, but he hadn't. Langdon was still there; he'd just taken his ropes off." Ashe shook his head. "Before the lawyer made them shut up, they were each claiming they did it on their own. The boy said he didn't kill Langdon. His sister said she did."

"What do you think?" John asked.

"I don't know." Ashe stood up. "I want a list of addresses.

Someone here saw something or knew something about at least one of them—Glassman, Ernst, Erwin or Siegel. That's too many murders to have no witnesses."

THE WOMAN who answered the door was enough like Gayle to identify her as a sister. She surveyed John briefly before her gaze traveled to his car.

"Oh! You must be Mr. Starek! Gayle has mentioned you."

His car anyway. John grinned. "Is she at home?"

"Yes, come in. We just finished dinner and are having coffee in the living room." She stepped back and gestured. "This way."

He followed her, hoping he'd have a chance to talk to Gayle alone. He hadn't thought about family dinner.

Gayle rose as he entered. "Mr. Starek."

Why hadn't he thought of a pretext for his visit? John nodded and smiled as she introduced him to her parents.

"You already know my friend, Lillian, and her husband, Willie."

The men shook hands. "Good to see you again," John said. "Congratulations on your marriage."

Willie wrapped an arm around his wife's shoulders and beamed. "Luckiest man on earth."

"Most blessed," Lillian said. "Right?"

"Absolutely." He kissed the top of her head. "I hear you're having a bit of trouble at the Empire, Starek."

That was an understatement. "Just a bit." He turned to Gayle. "I came by to see how you're doing and to beg you to stay on at the theater."

"I wouldn't dream of leaving," she said promptly. "Thank you for the bonus." Her eyes were sparkling. "I got it."

"Your car?" He grinned. "The Gray?"

"Yes, and it's wonderful." Gayle's smile lit up the room.

"We came over to go for a ride," Lillian said. "Come with us!"

"I'd love to."

"Now?" Gayle asked. "We were just leaving."

He nodded. "I can't wait to see it."

"She's a very good driver," Mrs. Wells said. "You'll be perfectly safe."

"I'm not a bit worried about that. Let's go!"

AS HE'D EXPECTED, Gayle was an excellent driver. She pointed out the merits of the Gray, describing the engine and suspension with enthusiasm. He enjoyed watching her pleasure.

He'd come for a purpose, though, so after ensuring the newlyweds in the backseat weren't listening, he said, "I saw Detective Ashe today. He told me about your brother-in-law."

A flash of anger crossed her face. "That's so ridiculous. Michael's suspended, and Ruth is pregnant."

He blinked at that, and she gave a rueful laugh. "Sorry. I'm just so upset. We should have said something right away, but we didn't, and then Jesse Erwin and Mr. Langdon were killed, and it was too late. Now Detective Ashe thinks I'm guilty of every crime from theft to murder, and he thinks Michael covered up evidence."

"Michael's suspended?" Lillian leaned forward, her voice shocked. "What did I miss?"

"You can't tell anyone!" Gayle said. "Especially not Ruth. Michael wants to see what happens first—if he's going to lose his job completely or just get demoted."

"That's terrible! Why does the detective think you're guilty?"

Gayle pulled the car to the side of the road and turned to face her friend. "Because I've been in the wrong place at the wrong time, over and over, and I keep bad company."

Lillian smirked. "Me?"

"Yes, and he's been looking for you." Gayle glanced at Willie. "I know you put pressure on Langdon—Siegel—to get me the job, Lillian. Is that why he pushed you into the street? So you wouldn't reveal his identity?"

"Siegel! That was it. I couldn't remember his name." Lillian turned to her husband. "He ran the Purple Rose club. Do you remember that place in New York, in the basement of that school?"

He nodded. "Best music in town."

"That's the man who was killed at the Empire. He was working as the manager there and using a different name."

Willie shook his head. "Strange cover. What was he really up to?"

They were all quiet for a minute.

"I don't know," John said, "and if Ashe knows, he hasn't told me. Mostly, he comes to tell me that Gayle is a suspicious person."

She squeezed the steering wheel. "I am so mad about Michael. It's really unfair."

John rubbed the back of his neck. "I'd like to talk to him, but he'd better not come to the theater, and if he doesn't want his wife to know he's in trouble, we'd better not meet at his house. Can you set up a meeting for us?"

"This seems a bit conspicuous," John said. He'd expected a meeting in a park or dark restaurant, not a drugstore soda fountain.

"It's good enough, and if someone did see us here, it won't look clandestine." Brady lifted his soft drink. "If you have something to tell me, do it now. If you have evidence, tell Ashe. I'm not going to get in more trouble."

"I have a problem," John said, "and I don't want to talk to

Detective Ashe about it in case I'm wrong. It could be entirely unrelated to his murder investigation, and I don't want him to handle it. He's making a mess of what he's got now. A new theory every day, contradicting himself, boasting… How did he get to be a detective?"

"Money," Michael said, "and I don't have any. I was having to work my way up." His shoulders slumped. "What a mess."

"Would you be willing to look into this for me? I won't offer you money," he said hastily, "but I'll cover your expenses. If it works out, maybe you can keep your job."

Michael looked at him, brows lowered. "You swear it's entirely on the up-and-up?"

"Yes."

"Okay. Tell me."

TWENTY-SEVEN

It had been shockingly easy to get Michael Brady reinstated. For a little more money, he could have bought him a promotion. John knew he should feel guilty about contributing to the corruption of Chicago politics, but mostly, he felt stunned by how simple a transaction it had been. His grandfather must never know. With luck, Brady would never know, either. It was just an expense that had to be covered for the man to do the job, right?

John looked around the room. He'd tried to gather all the people on Michael's list, and Detective Ashe had brought the Fishers. Lillian and Willie sat with Gayle, slightly apart from the other employees. Wilkes and two of his projectionist crew stood in the back, just as they did in the line of duty. A few stagehands, musicians, and the heads of various departments sat on the blue buffet chairs. No one looked comfortable.

Detective Ashe was behaving civilly, probably to save face in front of his men, but every covert glance at Michael held animosity. John hoped he wouldn't take his resentment out on the sergeant later. In spite of his successful foray into private investigation, Brady was committed to being a career policeman.

Looking calm and comfortable, Michael moved to stand in front of the little audience. "It's been a long week for all of you," he said, "but you should be able to resume operations soon. Mr. Starek asked me to look into some thefts that have been occurring here at the theater."

John raised his brows. He'd expected Brady to thank people for coming and ease into the topic, as if it was a business meeting, but the man wasn't wasting any time.

"No doubt, some of the items were taken by guests of the theater. Some of the thefts, however, could only have been managed by people associated with the Empire. Staff or vendors."

There was some shifting, but no one spoke. Michael continued. "Any of the housekeeping or maintenance staff would be in a position to steal things, but some of the things weren't just stolen. Certain of the valuable items, including some Egyptian statues and vases, were replaced by mass-produced copies. With the popularity of such decorations, reproductions are easily procured, but it would take some familiarity with the items to arrange for the substitutions. In addition, they would have to know where to purchase those reproductions and sell the originals."

Everyone was listening intently. John watched their faces, wondering how much each of them knew. Probably, each of them knew bits and pieces, individual parts of the puzzle but not the whole.

"Acting on information received," Michael said, "I communicated with law enforcement agencies in New York and learned that Benjamin Jones, of the Tobler and Jones talent agency, was suspected of art fraud. He'd been using his clients—performers who traveled across the country—as unwitting couriers, sending and receiving packages of money, art, jewelry and other valuable items."

Michael cleared his throat and continued. "We do not believe those couriers were aware they were transporting stolen goods. One man they interviewed believed he was carrying cash as a bribe for the theater manager."

"Langdon!" Frank Bennet stood and dropped back into his chair. "Langdon was a thief?"

"Yes, a thief and murderer. Last month, a cleaning woman dropped one of the Egyptian statues—one of the real ones— and put it back in its place, hoping no one would see it. Later, the woman confessed to her supervisor, and Miss Ernst told Mr. Langdon that one of the statues had been damaged. We conjecture that he had already exchanged the statues, not noticing the crack, and that Miss Ernst did not tell him of the woman who broke it. She may have even caught him exchanging it. He acted quickly, brutally killing her before his own wicked crimes could be discovered."

John grinned. Michael had a bit of the showman in him, enjoying the dramatic retelling.

"But who killed him?" someone asked.

More people were stirring now, anxious to have the mysteries cleared up. Langdon was dead, after all, and Ernie was only the beginning of the story.

"The police in New York knew Hewitt Langdon as George Siegel, and among his other crimes, they connected him with an investigation into series of jewelry thefts that turned out to be something quite different. He ran a casino where women came to gamble. According to their informant, Siegel would help women sell their jewelry for gambling money. Sometimes they reported it as stolen, and sometimes he aided them in replacing the real jewelry with fakes."

Michael shook his head. "The one thing the police kept saying about him was that he didn't stick with things. A little theft, a little gambling, a little fraud…the only thing he did really well was run clubs. He had a knack for setting up speakeasies and drawing crowds. His last one was the best. It was in the basement of a school, two stories below street level, accessed through a restaurant a block away. He leased it from a man who had no legal right to it—an architect who knew all the old tunnels and secret passages under the buildings and streets of New York."

He was a good storyteller. John glanced at the police officers standing at the doors. They knew who to watch.

"That man also told him of a place in Chicago, where a secret society was tapping into the old city's underground passages as they built their new headquarters. They would have access to the hotel across the street and points beyond. If Siegel ever wanted to expand his operations, he could set him up in the ritziest joint in town."

The Palace. They'd named it the Palace, and it was under the Empire. John hadn't believed it until Michael had shown him, taking him in through the theater's back staircase. It spiraled up the entire building and three stories below ground, opening into an elegant club, with casino tables, a bandstand and dance floor, a bar, and dozens of small tables. The decor mimicked that of the theater. The main entrance to the speakeasy was from a restaurant in the Halstead House, with smaller exits leading to a laundromat and an all-night diner.

"Langdon took foolish chances," Michael went on, "with ambitions beyond his abilities. He hung around the edges of the mob in New York, thinking he was working his way to the top. He let them have pieces of some of his casinos and clubs, in exchange for money and protection. But one day, he fenced an expensive necklace belonging to Dutch Schultz's girlfriend, and he was caught. He took as much cash as he could carry and left town."

"He contacted his old friend the architect, and he started laying the groundwork for setting up a club here, under the Empire. His timing was good. The Empire was in turmoil, having lost most of its staff when Mr. Starek took over. It was easy for him to get hired in the perfect position to run his club.

He saw it as just the beginning. Capone and his crew had gone to ground up north. Siegel had plans to set up his own organization."

"The cleaning women weren't hysterical!" Miss Larsen exclaimed. "They heard music and voices and people on the stairs, and no one had believed them."

Michael nodded. "No doubt, Siegel was pleased to find that he had inherited a competent assistant when he took the job as manager. He failed to recognize her ambition, however, or her growing resentment. She confided her frustrations to her young brother, who devised a plan to get Langdon out of the way, leaving the job open for Miss Fisher."

All heads turned toward the Fishers, sitting together under the watchful eye of a burly officer. The boy stared vacantly at a painting of an elephant. Eugenia, chin lifted, was watching Michael.

"On the day before Siegel killed Miss Ernst, James Fisher abducted him and drove him out to an old family cabin. He locked him up and went home to tell his sister what he'd done. We don't know what passed between them, but we do know Miss Fisher did not drive up to rescue her boss. She left him there, and when Miss Ernst was killed the next day, she believed it was an accident. The county police have located a farmer who came across Langdon walking down the road, the very night he was kidnapped. The farmer gave him a ride into the city. Langdon gave him a fifty-dollar bill for his trouble.

"What happened next is not quite clear. He found somewhere to spend the night, maybe somewhere in the theater or with a friend. In the morning, he killed Miss Ernst and returned to his prison. According to the testimony of James Fisher, Langdon was in the cabin when he brought food and water the following day. When Miss Lillian Nagle accused Langdon of trying to push her in front of a streetcar a week later, and the police started investigating Miss Ernst's death and Langdon's disappearance, Miss Fisher sent her brother to check on their captive. According to her brother, he was there, apparently content. We have since found evidence that he had a car nearby and could come and go at will through a crawl space hatch under the cabin."

"Did he kill Erwin?" Chester Klee asked. He leaned back in the banquet chair, rocking slightly. Art Hadley sat next to him, frowning.

Michael ignored the question. "As I said, he was an ambitious man. It suited him to be invisible for a while, free to make plans and travel at night, hiding in the corridors and empty rooms at the Empire. He created mischief, continuing to steal and planting evidence on other people."

He'd planned to incriminate Gayle, out of malice or because she was an easy target.

"Just two days ago, the New York police told us something that helped put all the pieces together. They believed that when Siegel left New York, he had two other men with him. One of those men was Henry Glassman, who had played at some of his establishments. They didn't know who the other man was." Michael flashed a smile. "I do. Glassman, in his own words, got religion. He didn't want to get his buddies in trouble, so he warned Siegel ahead of time that he was going to confess. He found a minister and made an appointment, but Siegel got to him before then, pushing him into the path of an oncoming streetcar."

"So, did he kill Erwin, too?" Klee asked again.

"Jesse Erwin figured it out on his own," Michael said, "based on comments made by people who had visited Siegel's nightclub in New York. Something I should have realized earlier. One of those people said Siegel's club had the best music in town. But you, Mr. Bennet, said Siegel—Langdon—was tone deaf. I wasn't sure if you meant that literally or not, so I asked around. Apparently, it was well-known among the musicians. The man really did have no business hiring Miss Wells. No wonder you were annoyed."

Klee and Hadley exchanged glances, shifting restlessly. Gayle tapped her foot, glaring at her brother-in-law.

"Erwin figured it out," Michael repeated, "and he was a power-hungry man. Now you had two loose cannons in your life, didn't you, Bennet? Siegel was running around, out of control. You'd come out here with him to start a new club. A really classy one, under the Empire movie palace. You had solid covers, with real jobs at the Empire and apartments at the Halstead house that gave you access to the club day and night. It was a cakewalk for you, if only Siegel would stop dabbling in theft and forgery, extortion, and trying to set up his own criminal organization. He'd already killed two people. He stayed with you that first night after he was kidnapped, didn't he? You gave him a ride back to the cabin. And I'd wager he came back several times to talk to you. When you told him Erwin was blackmailing you, he said he'd take care of it."

He paused. All eyes were on Bennet, who sat rigid, jaw clamped.

"You must have been angry that Siegel was botching your plan. You just wanted to run your speakeasy and be left alone." Michael's voice was sympathetic. "Was it Siegel's own gun you used to shoot him?" He waited for an answer, but Bennet didn't respond. "You knew where to dump his body—right back where the Fishers had left him, so they would be blamed. And then you had to kill Jesse Erwin right away, so Siegel would be blamed."

"But he had an alibi," Gayle objected. "He was with me!"

Michael shook his head. "No, he was behind you. He set you to playing a long piece of music, quietly left the room, met Erwin by prearrangement, killed him, and returned to the rehearsal room. You just played away, not knowing he was gone. It was a risk, but he was desperate. And if you had turned around to find him gone, he would have made some excuse. We had no reason to think he had a motive to kill Erwin."

Gayle was pink. "I'm sure I would have noticed if he'd left."

"You were occupied with the music," Michael said, "and possibly inclined to ignore him." He turned back to Bennet. "Did I miss anything?"

The man didn't speak. When the police officers grasped his arms, he rose easily and didn't resist. The others watched him go, silent, until the doors shut behind him.

Michael regarded them. "We aren't necessarily interested in prosecuting everyone who worked at the Palace, if any of you are willing to give testimony to the setup there. You can find me at the station later if you want to talk." He nodded, obviously finished.

The staff members disappeared, but John lingered, hoping to talk to Gayle after she said goodbye to her friends. Ashe had disappeared with the Fishers and the officers who took Bennet, and Michael was talking to a group of policemen across the room.

She finally approached him, smiling faintly. "That was exciting, wasn't it? I wish Ruth had been here."

"Ruth? Oh!" John chuckled. "Your sister. Would she have been proud of her husband?"

"Yes. It was quite a performance, wasn't it?" She tipped her head and looked at him. "You already knew, didn't you? That's why you wanted to talk to him that day, and he told you what he was going to reveal today, too."

"You're quite a detective, too," he said. "Yes, I did know. I wanted to talk to him about the thefts, mostly, but there were other things that seemed to go together, like that Zech and the illusionist with their packages. When the insurance man said the Egyptian statues were fakes…I thought it had to be something to do with Langdon."

"Well, we all thought everything was Langdon's doing, and most of it was!" Gayle rubbed her nose. "I just couldn't figure out the rest of it, and I thought Mr. Bennet was with me while Jesse was killed. He was my alibi!"

"You were his alibi, too," John said.

She shivered. "I'm glad it's over. Do you think you'll be able to open up again soon? I'd like to get back to work."

"I hope so, but I'm back to where I started, looking for new staff. It's going to take a while." He smiled at her. "At least I don't need a new chief organist."

Her eyes sparkled. "Do you mean that? You're promoting me?"

"Well, there's not a lot of competition for the post," he teased, "so I guess I'm stuck with you."

"You won't regret it. Thank you!" She gave him an impulsive hug and stepped back, blushing. "Sorry. I was excited."

"I don't mind a bit," John said. "Feel free to get excited as often as you like." He touched her elbow, steering her out of the way of the police officers clearing the room. "Would you…I can't exactly ask you out to a movie right now, but would you like to go out to dinner some evening soon? Maybe out dancing?"

"At a legal, respectable place that doesn't serve alcohol?" she asked.

"If I can find one," he said. He looked down at her bright, laughing eyes and felt happier than he had in months. He'd brought all kinds of treasures into the theater, but this one had found her own way in. And if things worked out as John hoped, this treasure would be where his heart was.

It was a slight divergence from the actual meaning of that passage from Matthew, but he liked the sound of it. He'd need to brush up on his Scripture memorization if he wanted to woo the organist. He needed to reexamine his childhood faith, too. That wasn't just for Gayle, though; it was time to grow up and talk to God again, as a man and not a child.

John watched Gayle as she shared the news with her friends. Lillian squealed and flung her arms around Gayle. Willie beamed. John would be a part of that group, some day. He was sure of it.

ABOUT THE AUTHOR

After 40 years of wandering (but always in lovely places and not in a descrt), **Cathe Swanson** has recently returned to her childhood home and family in Minnesota. In the summer, she and her husband enjoy spending time with their grandchildren and being outdoors, gardening, hiking, birdwatching, and kayaking. The long winters are perfect for writing books, playing games, reading, and indoor hobbies. Cathe's been a quilter and teacher of quiltmaking for over 25 years and enjoys just about any kind of creative work, especially those involving fiber or paper.

Everything inspires new books! A lifelong love of quilting, Cathe's Swedish heritage and an interest in genealogy led to The Glory Quilts series, and The Hope Again series is inspired by her life in the Midwest and experiences with the elderly, the military, and inner-city ministry. As a child of the sixties, she's having fun writing about hippies and the Jesus People movement in the Serenity Hill series.

Cathe writes books with creative plots and engaging characters of all ages, to glorify God and entertain and bless readers. Her heartwarming stories will make you laugh and make you cry – and then make you laugh again.

        facebook.com/CatheSwanson
        instagram.com/CatheSwanson
        pinterest.com/catheswanson
        bookbub.com/authors/cathe-swanson
        amazon.com/author/catheswanson
        goodreads.com/CatheSwanson

ALSO BY CATHE SWANSON

The Hope Again Series

Baggage Claim

Snow Angels

Long Shadows

Hope for the Holidays

Home Run

The Road Home (Spring 2022)

Christmas at the Unity Plenkiss

The Glory Quilts Series

Always and Forever

Matched Hearts

The Serenity Hill Series

Season of Change

Potato Flake Christmas

Murder at the Empire

Betwixt Two Hearts

BOOKS IN THE EVER AFTER MYSTERIES
SERIES

The Last Gasp by Chautona Havig
A Giant Murder by Marji Laine
When the Pilot Falls by April Hayman
Murder at the Empire by Cathe Swanson
The Lost Dutchman's Secret by Rebekah Jones
The Nutcracker's Suite by Chautona Havig
Silencing the Siren by Denise L. Barela
Slashed Canvas by Liz Tolsma

THE LOST DUTCHMAN'S SECRET

A SNEAK PEEK AT THE NEXT EVER AFTER MYSTERY!

REBEKAH JONES

ONE

Dorothy Hodges sat on the rough wooden chair by the tiny fire and pulled her mending into her lap. She had already tidied the small, three room shack that she shared with her father; breakfast things had been put away, Dorothy's little corner of books set to rights, and the dirt floor swept.

Her father, Joseph, sat at the table he had made decades before, his narrow eyes made narrower still as he squinted at the animal emerging from the wood that he held in his rough hands. His gray, scraggly hair, parted in the middle, hung well past his ears, while his curly beard marked with patches of pure white, seemed to bury most of his features. Even Dorothy, who didn't remember him without a beard, couldn't help but notice it.

His clothes hung about him, limp and careless; especially his miner's shirt, now long out of date and splattered with decades old wax. Dorothy saw a fresh tear on the lower edge of his sleeve while she looked at him, but she knew that he wouldn't let her mend it.

Tossing one of her golden braids out of her way, she bent her attention again to the mending on her lap, glancing toward the man at the table every once in a while. At twenty-five years old, she might have looked her age if she hadn't looked so out of time with her ankle length striped skirt, pleated and faded shirtwaist, and wide belt wrapped around her waist. Only her shoes, when she wore them, looked like they had actually been manufactured in the current decade.

Dorothy raised her thread to her teeth, but stopped short when she heard a man's voice outside. He scolded at the surrounding desert quite savagely. Dorothy looked at her father in alarm, but he just kept at his carving.

"That sounded like Mr. Sinclair, Father." She ordered the tremor from her voice.

Her father nodded. "So, it does."

Another growl outside sent her heart racing faster. "He'll be at the door within the minute."

"I imagine so." He didn't change his position, his expression, or even look at her.

Dorothy glanced around, wondering if it would be feasible to make an escape. Even if she ran to her room, she had no door and nothing to hide behind.

I'm not a child. I can face my fears.

She didn't have the time to consider further. Charles Sinclair, a large man with a further imposing presence and unnaturally soft voice, entered the shack without any pretense of knocking or asking permission. His dark, slicked back hair and upright bearing showed marked contrast to the woodcarver at the table, though there couldn't have been much difference in their ages. Where Dorothy's father stooped, the other stood tall. Where the former squinted, the latter held his eyes wide open. Where Joseph had grown wrinkled and gray, Charles seemed to exude youth and color.s

Dorothy could never help the comparison and only dropped her eyes back to her mending, when the newcomer grinned in her direction.

"Joe!" Dorothy quailed at the sound of his voice and

winced at the familiar greeting. "Pleasant to see you and your lovely daughter! How is the carving today?"

Dorothy looked up again as her father shook his weathered head.

"This little fella's givin' me trouble, but he'll turn out all right in the end, I reckon."

Charles Sinclair lay one of his large hands on the table and leaned over the small figurine. "It's a dog, isn't it?"

"A kai-ote. I suppose that's a dog, but they *are* pretty different."

Charles Sinclair nodded. "I see, I see. One should be exact." He pulled out a chair and Dorothy just caught a gleam in his eyes as he sat down. "Have you sold any carvings lately?"

Dorothy's father glanced up sharply. "A few down in Mesa."

"That's good. That's good."

They continued in silence for a few moments and Dorothy took a deep breath. Her hands trembled too much to properly continue her mending.

"I'm here for my money, Joe." He spoke the words quietly in the silent room, but Dorothy's heart still began pounding more swiftly.

"I know you are." Her father kept his gaze locked on the coyote.

"Should I have noticed it lying around somewhere by now? Did I miss something, Joe?"

"I don't imagine so."

Charles Sinclair stood, clasping his hands together. "Where's my money, Joe?"

He still didn't stop carving. "I don't have it."

"You don't have it. You..." The man glanced in Dorothy's direction and let the sentence die. He tried again. "You asked for another month, Joe. It's been another month."

"I know."

"You sold some of your carvings."

"I did, in fact."

"Then *where* is my money?"

The woodcarver didn't once raise his head. "Dorothy has to eat."

Charles Sinclair sighed, then leaned on the table beside the other man. "Look here, Joe. I can't keep coming up here. My automobile won't even make it—I had to walk a long way through cacti and brush just to reach you. What's more, this is the tenth time that you have been unable to deliver. You borrowed from me; it's time to pay your debt."

"I know." Dorothy's father nodded gravely. "Can't do it though. I don't have it yet, but I'll get it."

Dorothy squeezed her eyes shut. When she opened them, Charles Sinclair had straightened, his hands in his pockets.

"All right, Joe." He nodded. "All right. I'll give you more time. I'll give you until Saturday."

"Saturday week?"

"No. Saturday in five days."

Dorothy held her breath. *We'll never have it. Never.*

Charles Sinclair watched the coyote a moment longer before he spoke again. "Do you know the Dance Pavilion down at Apache Junction?"

"I reckon that I do."

"Good. Because I can't keep wandering through the desert all the time. Bring the money to the Pavilion on Saturday. One of my sons will be there to receive it."

"Can't." Dorothy's father shook his head. "I'm too busy."

Charles Sinclair's face darkened, his eyes narrowing, but only Dorothy saw it as her father never looked up.

"Does Dorothy know the way?"

Dorothy jumped.

"I reckon."

"Good." He nodded toward her, as if to tell her she couldn't argue. "Send her."

Dorothy's heart pounded harder. *Please, Father. Don't agree to send me. Say you'll find a way to go yourself.*

Her father, however, nodded, still focused on the coyote. "She'll be there."

"Good." Charles Sinclair picked up a wood shaving, rubbing it between his fingers. He bent lower beside the woodcarver. "I need my money, Joe. I need my money."

The other man nodded once more. "I know. You'll get it. Soon."

Made in the USA
Middletown, DE
07 April 2022

63659374R00142